格雷的老爸

格雷的爷爷

格雷的老妈

格雷的"死党"
——罗利

格雷的弟弟
曼尼

DIARY

of a Wimpy Kid

小屁孩日记④

—— 偷鸡不成蚀把米

［美］杰夫·金尼 著

朱力安 译

格雷的哥哥
——罗德里克

格雷

· 广州 ·

广东省出版集团

新世纪出版社

本书简体中文版由美国Harry N. Abrams公司通过中国Creative Excellence Rights Agency独家授权

版权合同登记号：19-2009-054号

图书在版编目（CIP）数据

小屁孩日记④：偷鸡不成蚀把米 /（美）杰夫·金尼著；朱力安译. —2版. —广州：新世纪出版社，2012.6（2016.6重印）

ISBN 978-7-5405-4219-1 / 03

Ⅰ. 小…　Ⅱ. ①杰…　②朱…　Ⅲ. 日记体小说—美国—现代　Ⅳ. I712.45

中国版本图书馆CIP数据核字（2009）第200727号

出　版　人：孙泽军
选题策划：林　铨　王小斌
责任编辑：王小斌　傅　琨　华　丽
责任技编：王建慧

小屁孩日记④——偷鸡不成蚀把米
XIAOPIHAI RIJI④——TOUJI BUCHENG SHIBAMI
　　〔美〕杰夫·金尼　著　朱力安　译

出版发行：新世纪出版社
　　　　　（广州市大沙头四马路10号　邮政编码：510102）
经　　销：全国新华书店
印　　刷：湛江南华印务有限公司
开　　本：890mm×1240mm　1/32
印　　张：7　　字　　数：135千字
版　　次：2010年1月第1版　2012年6月第2版
印　　次：2016年6月第28次印刷
定　　价：18.50元

质量监督电话：020-83797655　购书咨询电话：020-83781545

"小屁孩之父"杰夫·金尼致中国粉丝

中国的"哈屁族"：

你们好！

从小我就对中国很着迷，现在能给中国读者写信真是我的荣幸啊。我从来没想过自己会成为作家，更没想到我的作品会流传到你们的国家，一个离我家十万八千里的地方。

当我还是个小屁孩的时候，我和我的朋友曾试着挖地洞，希望一直挖下去就能到地球另一端的中国。不一会儿，我们就放弃了这个想法（要知道，挖洞是件多辛苦的事儿啊！）；但现在通过我的这些作品，我终于到中国来了——只是通过另一种方式，跟我的想象有点不一样的方式。

谢谢你们让《小屁孩日记》在中国成为畅销书。我希望你们觉得这些故事是有趣的，也希望这些故事对你们是一种激励，让你们有朝一日也成为作家和漫画家。我是幸运的，因为我的梦想就是成为一个漫画家，而现在这个梦想实现了。不管你们的梦想是什么，我都希望你们梦想成真。

我希望有朝一日能亲身到中国看看。这是个将要实现的梦想！

希望你们喜欢《小屁孩日记》。再次感谢你们对这套书的喜爱！

杰夫

A Letter to Chinese Readers

Hello to all my fans in China!

I've had a fascination with China ever since I was a boy, and it's a real privilege to be writing to you now. I never could have imagined that I would become an author, and that my work would reach a place as far from my home as your own country.

When I was a kid, my friends and I tried to dig a hole in the ground, because we hoped we could reach China on the other side of the earth. We gave up after a few minutes (digging is hard!), but with these books, I'm getting to reach your country... just in a different way than I had imagined.

*Thank you so much for making **Diary of a Wimpy Kid** a success in your country. I hope you find the stories funny and that they inspire you to become writers and cartoonists. I feel very fortunate to have achieved my dream to become a cartoonist, and I hope you achieve your dream, too... whatever it might be.*

I hope to one day visit China. It would be a dream come true!

*I hope you enjoy the **Wimpy Kid** books. Thank you again for embracing my books!*

Jeff

有趣的书，好玩的书

夏致

　　这是一个美国中学男生的日记。他为自己的瘦小个子而苦恼，老是会担心被同班的大块头欺负，会感慨"为什么分班不是按个头分而是按年龄分"。这是他心里一道小小的自卑，可是另一方面呢，他又为自己的脑瓜比别人灵光而沾沾自喜，心里嘲笑同班同学是笨蛋，老想投机取巧偷懒。

　　他在老妈的要求下写日记，幻想着自己成名后拿日记本应付蜂拥而至的记者；他特意在分班时装得不会念书，好让自己被分进基础班，打的主意是"尽可能降低别人对你的期望值，这样即使最后你可能几乎什么都不用干，也总能给他们带来惊喜"；他喜欢玩电子游戏，可是他爸爸常常把他赶出家去，好让他多活动一下。结果他跑到朋友家里去继续打游戏，然后在回家的路上用别人家的喷水器弄湿身子，扮成一身大汗的样子；他眼红自己的好朋友手受伤以后得到女生的百般呵护，就故意用绷带把自己的手掌缠得严严实实的装伤员，没招来女生的关注反惹来自己不想搭理的人；不过，一山还有一山高，格雷再聪明，在家里还是敌不过哥哥罗德里克，还是被耍得团团转；而正在上幼儿园的弟弟曼尼可以"恃小卖小"，无论怎么捣蛋都有爸妈护着，让格雷无可奈何。

　　这个狡黠、机趣、自恋、胆小、爱出风头、喜欢懒散的男孩，一点都不符合人们心目中的那种懂事上进的好孩子形象，奇怪的是这个缺点不少的男孩子让我忍不住喜欢他。

　　人们总想对生活中的一切事情贴上个"好"或"坏"的标签。要是找不出它的实在可见的好处，它就一定是"坏"，是没有价值的。

单纯的有趣，让我们增添几分好感和热爱，这难道不是比读书学习考试重要得多的事情吗？！生活就像一个蜜糖罐子，我们是趴在桌子边踮高脚尖伸出手，眼巴巴地瞅着罐子的孩子。有趣不就是蜂蜜的滋味吗？

翻开这本书后，我每次笑声与下一次笑声之间停顿不超过5分钟。一是因为格雷满脑子的鬼主意和诡辩，实在让人忍俊不禁。二是因为我还能毫不费劲地明白他的想法，一下子就捕捉到格雷的逻辑好笑在哪里，然后会心一笑。

小学二年级的时候我和同班的男生打架；初一的时候放学后我在黑板上写"某某某（男生）是个大笨蛋"；初二的时候，同桌的男生起立回答老师提问，我偷偷移开他的椅子，让他的屁股结结实实地亲吻了地面……我对初中男生的记忆少得可怜，到了高中，进了一所重点中学，大多数的男生要么是专心学习的乖男孩，要么是个性飞扬的早熟少年。除了愚人节和邻班的同学集体调换教室糊弄老师以外，男生们很少再玩恶作剧了。仿佛大家不约而同都知道，自己已经过了有资格耍小聪明，并且耍完以后别人会觉得自己可爱的年龄了。

如果你是一位超过中学年龄的大朋友，欢迎你和我在阅读时光中做一次短暂的童年之旅；如果你是格雷的同龄人，我真羡慕你们，因为你们读了这本日记之后，还可以在自己的周围发现比格雷的经历更妙趣横生的小故事，让阅读的美好体验延续到生活里。

要是给我一个机会再过一次童年，我一定会睁大自己还没有患上近视的眼睛，仔细发掘身边有趣的小事情，拿起笔记录下来。亲爱的读者，不知道当你读完这本小书后，是否也有同样的感觉？

片刻之后我转念一想，也许从现在开始，还来得及呢。作者创作这本图画日记那年是30岁，那么说来我还有9年时间呢。

一种简单的快乐

刘恺威

我接触《小屁孩日记》的时间其实并不长，是大约在一年多以前，我从香港飞回横店时，在机场的书店里看到了《小屁孩日记》的漫画。可能每一个人喜爱的漫画风格都不太一样，比如有人喜欢美式的、日系的、中国风的，有人注重写实感的，而我个人就比较偏向于这种线条简单的、随性的漫画，而且人物表情也都非常可爱。所以当时一下子就被封面吸引住了，再翻了翻内容，越看越觉得开心有趣，所以立刻就买下了它。

说实话，我并不认为《小屁孩日记》只是一本简单的儿童读物。我向别人推荐它的时候也会说，它是一本可以给大人看的漫画书，可以让整个人都感受到那种纯粹的开心。可能大家或多或少都会有这样的感受，当我们离开学校出来工作以后，渐渐的变得忙碌、和家人聚在一起的时间越来越少，也无法避免地接收到一些压力和负面情绪，对生活和社会的认知也变得更加复杂，有时候会感觉很累，心情烦躁，但如果真的自问为什么会这么累，究竟在辛苦追求着什么的时候，自己却又没有真正的答案……这并不是说我对成年后的生活有多么悲观，但像小孩子一样简单的快乐，确实离成年人越来越远了。但当我在看到《小屁孩日记》的时候，我却突然间想起了自己童年时那种纯真、简单的生活，这也是我决定买下这本漫画的原因之一。看《小屁孩日记》会让我把自己带回正轨，审核自己，检查一下自己最近的情绪、状况，还是要回到人的根本——开心。

　　我到现在也喜欢随手画一些小屁孩的画像来送给大家，这个也是最近一年来形成的习惯，因为自己大学读的是建筑，平时就喜欢随手画些东西，喜欢上小屁孩之后就开始画里面的人物，别看这个漫画线条简单，但想要用最简单的线条画出漫画里那种可爱的感觉，反而挺花功夫的。除了小屁孩这个主角之外，我最喜欢画的就是他的弟弟。弟弟是个特别爱搞鬼的小孩，而且长着一张让人特别想去捏他的脸。这兄弟俩的故事经常会让我想起我跟我妹妹的关系，我妹妹小时候也总是被我"欺负"，比如捏她的脸啊、整蛊她啊，但如果遇到了外人欺负妹妹，自己绝对是第一个站出来保护她的人。

十一月

<u>星期一</u>

　　罗德里克的狂欢派对已经过去一周了，大概已经尘埃落定，我也就不再担心爸妈会逮到我们了。不过，还记得我们调包过的那个洗手间房门么？好吧，我是彻底把它给忘得一干二净了，直到今晚这茬儿才被提起。

　　那会儿罗德里克正在楼上我的房间里烦我，然后眼看老爸就走进了洗手间。几秒钟之后，老爸说了一句话，吓得罗德里克大气不敢出。

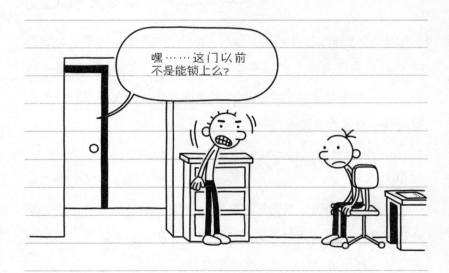

　　我心想这下完了。要是老爸知道了门的事情，那他知道狂欢派对就是迟早的事了。

　　但即便是这么顺理成章，水到渠成，老爸居然也没往深处想。

其实就算爸妈真知道了派对的事，这也不全是坏事，你说是吧？因为这样一来，罗德里克就会被禁足，这可是大好事一桩呀。所以要是我能找到办法既把风声走漏出去而又不会让罗德里克发觉，那就太完美啦。

星期二

今天，我收到了法国笔友马马杜的第一封来信。我决定调整心态，全力以赴认真对待笔谈这件大事。所以当我给马马杜回信的时候，我尽可能让自己显得像个良师益友。

亲爱的格雷： 　　十分荣幸能与你结识。 　　　　　　马马杜	亲爱的马马杜： 　　我十分确定"结识"应该写作"结实"①。 　　我看你真的应该好好学学英语。 　　　　　　诚挚的， 　　　　　　格雷

①　译注：原文中马马杜来信用词为"acquaintance"（结识），拼写无误，格雷却回信挑错，说应为"aquaintance"，无"c"，实为误导。

勒弗莱夫人真是古板，居然不让我们用E-mail来跟笔友通信。艾尔伯特·孟菲已经跟笔友书信来往好几回了，花了不少邮票钱呢。

亲爱的雅克： 你几岁了？	亲爱的艾尔伯特： 12.	亲爱的雅克： 哦。

邮资花费：14美元

星期五

晚上，罗利的父母外出用餐，他们给罗利雇了个保姆。

我实在搞不懂，就几个小时，罗利怎么就不能看好自己呢。不过你千万别误会，我可一点抱怨的意思都没有，因为罗利的保姆是茜特·希尔斯，她可是科罗斯兰高中最靓的女孩儿。

所以每当罗利的父母外出，我准会赶到罗利家，等着听故事。

我晚上8点到了罗利家门口。出门之前还特意喷了点罗德里克的古龙水，确保能万无一失地给茜特留下美好印象。

　　我敲了敲门，等着茜特过来开门。但来开门的居然是罗利家的胖邻居勒兰德，把全无防备的我当场吓个半死。

嗨！

啊！！

　　罗利的家长居然放着茜特不要，换了勒兰德来当保姆，真是令人难以置信。他们做这种傻事之前至少也该知会我一声啊。

　　一看茜特没来，我转身就往家走。不过罗利问我想不想多呆一会儿跟他和勒兰德一起玩《魔法与怪兽》的游戏。

　　我当时答应下来只是因为我以为那是某个电动游戏。后来我才知道这是一个用纸和笔还有一些特殊骰子来玩的游戏，而且还得运用点"想象力"什么的。

　　这游戏其实挺有趣的，主要是因为在《魔法与怪兽》的世界里，你可以做各种现实生活中不可能的事情。

回家后，我跟妈大谈特谈《魔法与怪兽》，还有勒兰德——绝佳的地下城守护者①。罗德里克无意中听到我谈起勒兰德，他告诉我们勒兰德是他们高中最呆的呆瓜。

不过这显然不足取信，因为说这话的人自己每周六晚上都躲在家得宝②的停车场里，往别人的车上扔自制呕吐物。所以我对罗德里克的话半信半疑。

① 译注：《魔法与怪兽》是一种像"龙与地下城"那样的魔幻类纸笔游戏，地下城守护者相当于一个维护规则、主持游戏的庄家。

② 译注：家得宝（The Home Depot）公司成立于1978年，是全球最大的家具建材零售商，美国第二大零售商。

星期三

　　我现在天天放学都跑去勒兰德家里玩《魔法与怪兽》游戏。今天我正要再去，就被妈在门口截住了。

　　老妈一直对这《魔法与怪兽》游戏满腹狐疑。

　　从她问我的问题来看，我猜她八成是怀疑勒兰德在教我和罗利什么巫术邪法之类的。所以，今天老妈说她要陪我去，看看我们到底在勒兰德家里玩什么。

　　我苦苦哀求老妈，叫她不要跟来，因为首先，我知道她是绝不会认可这个游戏中所涉及的暴力成分的。

　　其次，我知道，她要是在一旁，肯定会扫了大家的兴。

　　我哀求老妈不要来，反而让她更为怀疑。她现在是铁了心要来。

罗利和勒兰德对老妈跟我一起来这件事全然无视，完全没有放在心上。但我是没法尽兴了，因为在她面前玩，我感觉自己就像个呆瓜一样。

呃……我的巫师塔洛克念出了塔罗符文上的魔咒。

　　我以为老妈迟早会觉得无聊然后乖乖回家，但她一直杵在那里。当我正以为她终于挨不住要走的时候，老妈说她也想加入游戏。

　　尽管我一直在给勒兰德打眼色，示意他这么干是大错特错的，他还是开始为老妈创建人物了。

　　勒兰德创建好人物后，老妈说她想让她的游戏角色成为我的游戏角色的妈。

　　我急中生智，跟老妈说在《魔法与怪兽》中所有角色都是孤儿，所以她不能当我的妈。

　　老妈信了。不过她问勒兰德能否将她的人物名称定为"老妈"，勒兰德说"可以"。

这都能让她钻到空子，不得不佩服。不过她是彻彻底底毁了我后半场游戏。

尽管原则上老妈在游戏中并不是我的妈，但她处处显出老妈作风。

这会儿，我们的人物在一个酒馆里逗留，等待探子回来报信。我的矮人角色格林隆点了一品托的蜂蜜酒。蜂蜜酒是《魔法与怪兽》里一种类似啤酒的酒，我早猜到老妈是不会批准我喝酒的了。

最糟糕的还要数打仗的时候。你看，《魔法与怪兽》的精髓本来就在于尽可能多地杀怪兽，积累经验值，然后升级。

但我觉得老妈压根就没搞懂。

就这样不汤不水地过了一个小时，我决定不玩了。我收拾好东西，就跟老妈一起回家了。

回家路上，老妈句句不离《魔法与怪兽》，大谈特谈这个游戏可以如何提高我的"数学技能"之类的。我唯一指望的是，老妈千万别打算成为这个游戏的常驻玩家。因为我一有机会就会把"老妈"交到一群半兽人手里的。

星期四

今天放学后，老妈带我去了趟书店，几乎买遍了所有关于《魔法与怪兽》游戏的书。这趟肯定花了老妈不下200块大洋，但她一点都没有扣我的"母元"来抵偿。

我想我对老妈可能太先入为主了，让她加进我们的游戏团队不见得是坏事。她这不给我们买了好多书嘛！

我正想着把新买的书搬到勒兰德那儿去，忽然发现其中有诈。

原来老妈买这么些书其实是为了让我跟罗德里克一起玩《魔法与怪兽》。她说，这样一来我跟罗德里克可以沟通磨合一下。

老妈跟罗德里克说她想让他来充当地下城守护者，就像勒兰德在游戏里的角色一样。说完把那摞书往罗德里克床上重重一掷，让他立马研究上手。

　　在勒兰德家里当着老妈的面玩本来就够糟糕的了，但我知道，要是跟罗德里克一起玩那将是十倍的糟糕。

　　老妈对我跟罗德里克通过游戏互动这件事还十分上心，所以我看我是在劫难逃，不得不硬着头皮上了。我在房间里花了近一个小时来给新建人物取名字，比如"乔"和"鲍勃"之类的，确保罗德里克没法拿这些名字来开涮。

　　等我确保万无一失后，在厨房找到罗德里克，我们就开始游戏了。

　　这么快就完事了，我还真该感谢上苍。但愿老妈还留着购书发票以便退货。

星期五

　　老师们今年果然狠抓考试时交头接耳、偷看作弊的问题。之前说过代数预备班上我坐在艾力克斯·阿鲁达旁边，为此还暗自庆幸，还记得这事儿么？现在看来全是枉然。

　　李老师是代数预备班的老师，我估计她以前还教过罗德里克，因为这女人老像鹰隼一样死死地盯着我。

　　有时候我想啊，要是我有一颗玻璃假眼之类的玩意儿就好了。首先，可以用来在朋友身上玩些古灵精怪的把戏。

但我主要还是想用它来助我考试得高分。

上学头一天，我会让我的玻璃假眼往下聚焦，就像这样：

然后跑去跟老师说："老师，我来是想告诉你我有一只眼睛是玻璃做的假眼，所以请不要以为我在偷看别人的试卷。"

然后呢，考试时我就会让假眼往下聚焦在自己的卷子上，而真眼就用来瞅其他聪明仔的试卷。

这样我就能大抄特抄了！而且老师这么木，肯定看不出真假。

唉，可怜的孩子少了只眼啊。

不幸的是，我并没有这样一个玻璃假眼，所以今天代数预备班的随堂考试我挂了。要是老妈问我为什么考挂了呢，这就是我的最佳借口。

星期天

罗德里克最近老跟爸妈要钱，所以我猜一定是"母元"项目在他身上行不通。老妈试图让罗德里克多做家务来挣零花钱，但效果并不见得好。

老爸，是这么干么？

儿啊，你得先找块干净的抹布！

不过今晚，老妈灵机一动想出了新的工种好让罗德里克挣零花钱——学校给家里来信，说由于经费不足取消了音乐课程，所以改由家长自行安排家教。

老妈于是让罗德里克给我当家教，教我爵士鼓，她给他付学费。

老妈会有这个想法，大概是因为罗德里克最近四处吹嘘自己是一个"专业鼓手"。

有这么一种民间表演叫"社群滑稽剧"，也就是左邻右舍的家长上台逗趣耍宝，说一些个桥段。"社团滑稽剧"已经在当地剧院上演了快两周了。

前几天晚上，那个正规鼓手病了，罗德里克去顶了几天，赚了5美元。

我不知道当了回替补是不是就能让罗德里克跻身"专业鼓手"，不过这并不妨碍我沾他的光在女生圈子赢点名声。

当老妈敦促罗德里克开始给我上爵士鼓课的时候，罗德里克显得并不热衷。不过后来老妈说她会给罗德里克付课酬，10美元一节，她还说我可以呼朋引伴一块儿报名。

所以现在我就得动员一些人来加盟罗德里克的爵士鼓学会，但是我可以断言，这个爵士鼓学会要想有意思恐怕很难。

星期一

找不到任何人自愿报名参加，除了罗利——而且还是被我忽悠进来的。罗利一直说他想学打鼓，不过他想打的是仪仗队里的那种鼓。

我毫不含糊地跟罗利说，罗德里克将会在第四周的授课内容中涵盖所有相关内容，罗利听完激动不已。

　　而我唯一高兴的则是，以后不用独自一人去上爵士鼓课了。

　　罗利放学后就过来了，我们来到地下室，开始第一节课。罗德里克先教了我们一些相当基本的技法。

　　我们只有一个练习鼓和两支鼓棒，所以罗利只能委屈一下，用纸盘和塑料餐具来将就了。不过最后一个报名的人通常也就是这种待遇了，惯例如此嘛。

　　大概才过了15分钟，罗德里克接到了沃德的电话，于是第一节课就这样告一段落了。

17

看到我跟罗利这么快就回到楼上，老妈可不太乐意，她又把我们打发回地下室，说让罗德里克给我们布置完家庭作业我们才能上来。

星期二

　　今天，罗德里克又给我和罗利上了爵士鼓课。

　　好吧，罗德里克或许是一个好鼓手，但他绝不是一个好老师。我跟罗利已经尽量按足他教的技法来打了，但每次我们出差错，他都会很抓狂。

最后，他忍无可忍，就没收了我们的鼓棒。罗德里克坐回到他的爵士鼓旁，让我们留心看示范。然后他就开始了他那冗长的、而且跟授课内容全然无关的独奏。

当我跟罗利走出地下室回到楼上的时候，罗德里克甚至连眼睛都没有移开过爵士鼓。

不过我并不是在抱怨什么，因为在我看来，这样大家才能共赢嘛。

星期二

感恩节前一天有一篇历史作文要交，我最好开始严阵以待了。

老师们现在对我们交上去的作业严把质量关，所以我以前应付作业的方法已经不吃香了。

上个星期科学课有一篇作文要交，布莱克曼夫人让我们选一种动物来写，我就选了麋鹿。我也知道本该去图书馆查找资料研究一下的，不过我想着混过去就算了。

了不起的麋鹿

格雷·赫夫利

饮食：麋鹿吃很多、很多种东西，品类繁多，如果列表则嫌过长，这里就不一一罗列进本文里了。为了给大家节省时间，这里我只列出麋鹿不吃的东西。

泡泡糖　　　　金属　　　　匹萨饼

您的匹萨饼好了，先生。

哦不，不……我不吃匹萨饼。

尽管满大街都是麋鹿保护区，但麋鹿还是几乎绝种了。

可是我们比羚羊好闻多了。

噢.

我说的是死光①，没说你脏.

人人都知道麋鹿是从鸟进化过来的，就跟人一样。不过在进化中的某个环节，人们长出了手，而麋鹿这群倒霉蛋只长出了没用的角。

耶耶!

讨厌.

剧终

① 原文取的是 "stink"（臭）与 "extinct"（灭绝）的谐音。

其实我还觉得自己写得挺不错的。不过布莱克曼夫人想必是麋鹿专家之类的，因为她让我去图书馆查资料然后全文重写。

下一篇作文也绝非省油的灯。哈夫先生的课要求这篇作文得写一首关于20世纪初的诗歌，而我对历史和诗歌同样是一窍不通。所以我看我得开始啃啃书本了。

星期一

昨天我去罗利家下棋，最疯狂的事情发生了。当罗利去洗手间的时候，我发现有一些游戏代币从其他放游戏的箱子里露出一角。

我简直不敢相信自己的眼睛，因为这些游戏代币跟老妈发给我们的"母元"完完全全就是同一种币。

我点了点钞票，盒子里大概有$100,000，而且还是现金。

只消2秒钟，我就打定主意下一步该干什么了。

　　回到家后，我跑到楼上，把钱塞到我的床垫下面。我彻夜翻来覆去，思前想后，琢磨到底拿这些代币来做什么好。

　　我意识到老妈或许有一些防伪机制来辨别真假母元，所以决定今早小小试验一下。

　　我问老妈我能否兑现一些母元，这样一来我就可以买邮票来跟笔友通信。当我把那些游戏代币递给老妈的时候，着实紧张得要命。

但她眼都不眨就收下了"母元"。

真是走运得难以置信！这$100,000代币足够我用到高中毕业，甚至更久。我怀疑毕业后连工作都不用找了。

秘诀在于不要一次兑现太多，否则就穿帮了。

而且我还得记住偶尔也要实打实地挣一点母元，这样老妈就不会起疑心了。

不过有一点是可以肯定的，那就是我绝对不会用老妈刚给我的钱去买邮票。

我收到了笔友马马杜的照片，就在昨天的来信里。这张照片基本上扼杀了我给他回信的全部可能。

帅呆了

星期二

历史课的大作文明天就要交了，不过人们都说今晚会下一英尺厚的雪。这已经说了足足有一周了。

所以我还没费那劲开始写。

大概到了10:00左右，我窥探了一下窗外，看看到目前为止地上的积雪有多厚。当我拉开窗帘时几乎不敢相信自己的眼睛。

天啊，我还指望着明天能停课呢。我打开电视新闻看看怎么回事，但是气象播报员的说法跟三小时前说的完全不是一个版本。

鲍勃，这次好险，我们真是侥幸逃过一劫啊。

可不就是嘛，芭芭拉。哈哈哈。

　　也就是说，我得整整我的历史作文了。问题是现在已经太晚来不及去图书馆了，而家里又没有什么关于20世纪初的书。所以我得赶紧想点别的办法。

　　很快我就有了一个绝佳的点子。

　　老爸已经不下几百万次帮罗德里克渡过作文难关了。所以我看他也能帮帮我吧。

　　我跟老爸说了说我目前的处境，想着他会挺身而出，见义勇为。不过我猜老爸是在这个科目上吃过了苦头。

罗德里克肯定是听到了我跟老爸的对话，因为他让我跟他下楼去。

知道么，罗德里克初中时也上过哈夫先生，我现在的历史老师的课。原来罗德里克跟我上同一个年级的时候，哈夫先生给他们班布置过一模一样的作业。

罗德里克在他的杂物废品抽屉里翻了翻，找到了那篇旧文章。然后他说可以卖给我，售价5美元。

我跟他说我绝不会做这种事。

我得承认，这确实很诱惑。因为首先，罗德里克的作业都经过老爸的润饰加工，他的作文肯定是得过高分的。其次，老师只热衷于那些漂漂亮亮的透明塑料文件夹里的作文。

　　还有，我楼上的床垫下面还藏着一大叠的代币，可以用这些来支付给罗德里克。

　　但我做不到。我的意思是，虽然我曾经在小·测试上或其他时候抄过别人的作文，但是买别人的作文就另当别论，这可是上升到一个完全不同的层面了。

　　所以我决定振作起来，独自完成这篇作文。

　　我开始在电脑上做些调查研究，但就在午夜时分，可以想见的最糟糕的事情发生了：停电。

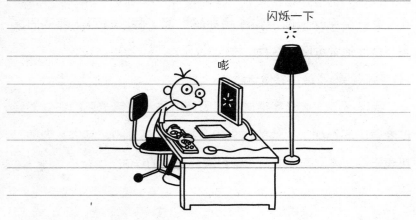

这下我知道自己是真的处在水深火热之中了。我要是不能交出这篇作文，我的历史课就得挂科了。所以尽管我不想这样，我还是得接受罗德里克出的价码。

　　我凑出$500代币，就到地下室来了。不过罗德里克可不会那么轻易放过我。

　　罗德里克说出他的最新价码，折合成母元是$20,000。我跟他说我没那么多，他翻过身去，又接着睡了。

　　那会儿我都急疯了。我上楼去抓了一大把千元大钞，然后拿着钱到罗德里克房里。我一手交钱，他一手交卷。对于自己的所作所为，我感到相当惭愧，但我尽量不去多想，然后睡了。

星期三

　　在上学途中的巴士上，我从包里拿出了罗德里克的作文。但我只看了一眼就发现大事不妙了。

首先，整首诗不是打印出来的，而是罗德里克手写的。

这时我才忽然想起来：罗德里克上高中之后，老爸才开始经手他的作文。也就是说，这篇作文是罗德里克自己写的。

我开始读这篇作文，看看是否还有可用之处。但显而易见的是：罗德里克在做研究方面比我还要糟糕。

百年之前①

罗德里克·赫夫利作

我时而坐下畅想，
关于我所不知的世界，
那时的地球究竟是怎生模样，在
一百年以前。

洞穴人是否骑着恐龙游走？
花朵是否伴着蝴蝶？
我们可以尽管猜想，但那已是
一百年以前。

我唯愿人们造出时间机器，
载着我回到从前，
去目睹那时的景象，在
一百年以前。

统治世界的是巨型蜘蛛？
荒漠是否流出甘泉？
我想知道那时的故事，在
一百年以前。

F ②来找我谈话！

我看我是得到教训了，在收买别人的作文方面——或者，至少是在收买罗德里克的作文方面。

① 原文押韵，为保持原诗风格，内容有所改动。
② F，即Fail，不合格。

第三节课渐行渐近，我还是交不出东西给哈夫先生。看来暑假得乖乖留校补习历史课了。

没想到更倒霉的还在后面呢。我放学一回家就看到老妈站在门口等我。

还记得我付给罗德里克的那叠钞票么？呃，罗德里克想将它们一次兑现，然后买一辆二手摩托车。不用说，老妈肯定看出破绽了，因为罗德里克连一块钱的母元都没赚到过。

罗德里克跟老妈招了他得到母元的途径，老妈就把我的房间搜了个遍，直到她在床垫下搜到了我藏的伪币。老妈十分清楚$100,000远远超过她发行流通母元的额度，所以她没收了我全部的钱，连我自己挣来的那些都没有放过。我看母元计划是寿终正寝了。

老实说，我还真的有种解脱的感觉。每晚都压着这么一大堆钞票睡觉，真让我紧张失眠。

老妈查出我这样蒙骗她，真是气坏了，惩罚是在所难免的了。不过我在吃饭前就轻巧地化解了。

星期四

今天是感恩节，还是一如既往，只是这次罗莱塔姨妈早来了两个小时。

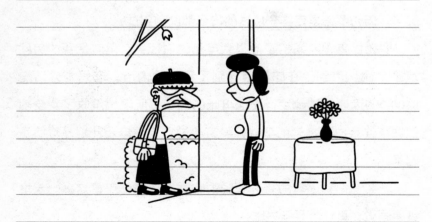

老妈每次都让我和罗德里克来"招待"她，也就是说让我们一直跟她说啊说直到其他家庭成员——登场为止。

光是为了谁先去跟她打招呼这个问题，我跟罗德里克还经历了有史以来最严重的一次大打出手。

　　到了11:00左右，其他家庭成员开始逐个亮相，来得最晚的是乔叔和他的孩子们，大概12:30才到的。

　　乔叔的孩子们全都这样跟老爸打招呼：

嗨，方克
姨妈①！

　　老妈觉得这么叫很别致，但老爸一口咬定是乔叔指使他们这

---

　　① 格雷的爸爸叫弗兰克·赫夫利（Frank Heffley），这里孩子们管他叫"方克姨妈"（Aunt Fwank），一来给他改了名，二来给他变了性。

33

么干的。

　　老爸跟乔叔之间还有些剑拔弩张，因为老爸还为乔叔上个感恩节的所作所为而气愤不已。那时候，曼尼才刚刚开始学着自己上厕所，一切都进展得不错。其实当时他已经有两周不需要尿布了。

　　不过自从乔叔跟曼尼说了几句话后，一切就天翻地覆了。

　　六个月之后曼尼才敢再次踏入洗手间。

　　自那以后，老爸每次换尿布，我都听到他小声地咒骂乔叔。

　　我们大概下午2点吃的饭，然后人们就到客厅去聊天。我可没什么说话的兴致，就跑去活动室打电子游戏了。

　　最后，我猜老爸也受不了那些亲戚，他就下楼去加工他的美国内战战场微缩模型了。不过他忘了关地下室的房门，乔叔就跟进来了。

乔叔貌似对老爸现在做的这个玩意很感兴趣，所以老爸就事无巨细地对他讲了一遍。

　　老爸还发表了一通长篇大论，讲第150军团和它在葛底斯堡战役中扮演的角色等等，还花了半个小时来描述整场战役。

　　不过我可不认为乔叔在留心听老爸的演说。

　　之后没过多久就散伙了。老爸上楼把暖气调高了，房里空气越来越闷，大家受不了就走光了。我们家几乎每年的感恩节都以这种方式草草收场。

十二月

记不记得我说过爸妈迟早会发现罗德里克的那次派对？今天就应验了。

老妈让老爸去取冲洗好的感恩节照片，当老爸回来的时候，一眼就可以看出他有点怒火中烧。

老爸手里的照片正是罗德里克的那次派对留下的写照。

这估计是罗德里克的某个朋友不经意间拍摄下来的，用的是老妈搁在音箱上面的架子上的相机。他拍下照片的那一刻，照片捕捉到了整个场面。

36

罗德里克还想抵赖一下，但照片里面什么都有了，一切否认都是徒劳。

老爸和老妈没收了罗德里克的车钥匙并罚他整整一个月不准出门。

他们连我都气上了，因为他们说我是罗德里克的"帮凶"。所以我也被牵连，被罚两周不准玩电子游戏。

星期天

自从发现罗德里克的派对后，老爸老妈一直对他严厉谴责。罗德里克通常一觉睡到第二天下午2点，但今天老爸一大早才8点就打发他起床了。

迫使罗德里克早起这对他来说实在是重大打击，因为罗德里克超爱睡觉。去年秋天有一次罗德里克一连睡了36个小时。

他从星期天晚上一直睡到星期二上午，而且浑然不知自己已经错过了人生中的整整一天，直到晚上才发觉。

嘿……周一晚间足球节目哪儿去了？

不过罗德里克似乎找到了一个迂回方法绕过这个8点新规矩。现在只要老爸一叫罗德里克起床，他就拽着铺盖卷上楼在沙发上接着睡，直到饭点。所以我看这个回合要算是罗德里克胜出。

星期二

老爸跟老妈这个周末又要出门，他们要把我跟罗德里克搁在爷爷家。他们说他们本打算让我们呆在家里的，但事实证明我们自己呆在家里是让大人放心不下的。

爷爷住在"休闲塔"一家老人院里。我跟罗德里克数月前曾在那里住过一周，那是整个暑假里最黑暗的日子。

曼尼则去奶奶家过周末。只要能跟他交换地方住，让我拿什么跟他换我都愿意。奶奶的冰箱里总是囤着苏打水、蛋糕之类的东西，她还装了有线电视，而且还开通了所有电影频道。

曼尼能去奶奶家住是因为曼尼是奶奶的最爱。你只消看看奶奶家冰箱就知道了，证据确凿。

　　不过如果有人指责奶奶偏心，她可绝不松口。

不仅仅是贴在冰箱上的照片，奶奶还把曼尼的画和其他东西挂得满屋都是。

奶奶保留的唯一一件我的真迹是我六岁时给她留的一张便条。那时我很生她的气，因为她饭前不肯给我吃雪糕，所以我写的是：

奶奶我恨你

这么多年来奶奶一直保留着那张字条，到现在还念念不忘。

我猜每个祖父母都有自己所偏爱的儿孙，可以理解，但爷爷也做得太出位了。

星期六

　　好吧，今天老爸老妈把我和罗德里克丢到爷爷家了，真是说到做到。

　　我开始找点办法自娱自乐一下，但是在爷爷的公寓里根本没有任何趣事可做，我只好坐下来跟他一起看电视。但爷爷连电视都不看。他只把电视机接到了大厅的闭路电视上。

　　只要一连看那么几个小时，你准会想发疯的。

好啊！巴利·格罗斯曼有时间去散步3小时，就是没空把我的吸尘器还给我！

　　大概到了下午5点，爷爷就给我们做饭了。爷爷会做一种很难吃的东西，叫"西洋菜沙拉"，这恐怕是你所尝过的最糟糕的食物了。

　　这基本上就是一些四季豆和黄瓜漂浮在整碗醋里。

罗德里克知道我最痛恨"西洋菜沙拉"，所以上次我们呆在爷爷家的时候，他无论如何都要把它往我盘子里堆。

我不得不坐在那里一口一口地拼命往下咽，以免伤害爷爷的感情。

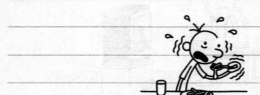

猜猜我清了一整盘沙拉后得到的奖励是什么？

晚餐时，爷爷又给我们上了沙拉，我装成好像在吃的样子。不过我其实只是趁他们不注意就把沙拉塞进我的兜里。

当凉冰冰的醋开始沿着我的腿往下流的时候，我觉得相当恶心。不过说真的，这可比把它们吃下去要好一千倍。

用餐过后我们三个来到厅里。爷爷有一堆老得掉渣的棋类游戏，他老是让我跟罗德里克陪他玩。

他有一款游戏叫"勇者无惧"，玩法是一个玩家念卡片，另一个玩家听完要忍住不笑。

我老是赢爷爷，主要是因为这些笑话在我听来根本不知所云。

我也经常赢罗德里克，不过这是因为他故意输的。每次轮到我念卡片的时候，他一定要含一大口牛奶。

到了晚上10:00，我准备睡觉了。不过罗德里克先霸了沙发，这就意味着我又得跟爷爷睡了。

我唯一能说的就是，如果爸妈是想给我一个教训，因为我包庇罗德里克而惩罚我的话，那他们的目的已经达到了。

星期天

　　罗德里克有一个很大的科学展览项目在圣诞节前要完成，看来这次爸妈是想让罗德里克自力更生了。

　　去年，罗德里克的科学展实验项目叫做"看暴力电影会使人们产生暴力想法吗？"

　　据我理解，大意是让人们去看恐怖片，看完让他们画画，如此来反映电影对他们产生的影响。

　　不过这其实只是一个借口，好让罗德里克和他的朋友们可以在第二天还要上学的情况下晚上还能大看恐怖片。

　　罗德里克的朋友们完成了电影观看这部分，但他们连一张图都没有画。到了科学展前夜，罗德里克还是什么都拿不出来。

　　所以我、老爸、老妈得要帮罗德里克脱险。老爸管作文打印和定稿，老妈管海报版展示架之类的，我就负责画一堆画。

　　我尽了最大努力来想象年轻人看了暴力电影后会画出什么来。

 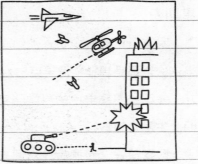

　　倒霉的是我的画居然还引起老妈的强烈反响，因为她看了我的画后说它们"令人不安"（大概是我装得太像了），所以往后这一年到头我都只准看老少咸宜的G级①电影。

　　不过真要说"令人不安"的话，你还真该看看曼尼那段日子里画出来的东西。

　　有一天晚上，罗德里克粗心大意把他的一张恐怖片的碟留在DVD机里面了。第二天曼尼过来开机看卡通的时候，看到的却是罗德里克的电影。

　　我偶尔见过几张曼尼那次看暴力电影之后所画的画，其中有几张足以让我晚上做噩梦。

　　① 按照美国电影分级制度，G指的是"general admission"，即老少咸宜。

星期二

老爸老妈为罗德里克的科学展项目定了最后期限，到今晚6:00的时候，罗德里克就该向他们汇报实验主题了。

但到了6:45，一切仍然不见起色。

罗德里克正在看一个电视节目，是关于宇航员以及他们在太空长期逗留后的变化的。节目说当这些宇航员回到地球的时候，他们竟然比离开地球的时候长高了。

　　原因就是太空中没有重力，所以他们的脊椎得到解压之类的。

　　嗯，这恰好给罗德里克提供了他要找的点子。

　　罗德里克跟爸妈说他要做一个关于"零重力"对人体脊椎之影响的科学实验。根据罗德里克的夸夸其谈来看，他的实验结果将造福全人类。

　　老爸听后为之一振。或许只是因为罗德里克完成了第一个任务，老爸觉得松了口气罢了。不过当他让罗德里克去倒垃圾的时候，我猜他就开始看出有点事与愿违了。

动不了，我正在做研究呢。

星期三

昨天上学时候，他们说冬季才艺秀的选拔赛有通知了。

我一听说这个就想到了一个绝佳的喜剧桥段，可以由我跟罗利来演。不过我得承认我编剧的真实动机是为了给自己找个借口跟霍莉·希尔斯搭讪，她可是我们年级人气最高的女生，还是茜特·希尔斯的妹妹。

49

剧终

致谢
剧本 - 格雷·赫夫利
导演 - 格雷·赫夫利
老爸 - 格雷·赫夫利
老妈 - 霍莉·希尔斯
狗孩 - 罗利·杰弗逊

我给罗利看了剧本，不过他似乎对这个点子缺乏热情。

猛地一推

我本可以把罗利捧红的啊，我还想着他会感恩戴德呢。不过就像老妈常说的，有些人就是不知足，有什么办法呢。

星期四

罗利去别处找了个搭档来参加才艺秀。他要跟他空手道班的一个同学，叫斯科提·道格拉斯的一起表演魔术。

你要是想知道我是否心存嫉妒的话，我就跟你明说吧：斯科提·道格拉斯是个一年级学生，所以罗利跟他玩的话，在学校里不被围殴就算走运了。

他们搞的这个才艺秀是小学、初中、高中合办的。也就是说罗德里克和他的乐队要跟罗利和斯科提·道格拉斯同台竞技了。

　　罗德里克为了这个才艺秀开足了马力。他的乐队从来没有在人前表演过，所以他们把这次处女秀视作人前露脸的大好时机。

　　罗德里克还在禁足期间，不过规矩说的是他不能出门，没说别人不能来家里找他。所以他的乐队可以每天过来在地下室里排练。我猜老爸开始后悔当初没弄个别的狠招来惩罚他了。

啪咚、砰、锵、嘭

　　不过要是罗德里克的乐队真想在这次才艺秀中拿到名次的话，他们最好把这个当回事，搞点真正的音乐。因为他们上两次排练的时间都浪费在拿周末刚买的脚踏回声效果器来胡闹上了。

星期五

老爸提前两周给罗德里克解禁了，因为他听水不湿乐队的排练听到崩溃，已经快神志不清了。所以今晚罗德里克去他朋友沃德家过周末。

罗德里克不在家，也就意味着地下室现在是我的地盘了。所以我邀请罗利来家里过夜。

我跟罗利买了好些糖果和苏打水，罗利还把他家的手提电视带过来了。我们甚至还把罗德里克的一些恐怖电影弄到手了，万事俱备，只欠东风了。不过就在那时老妈带着曼尼下楼来了。

老妈把曼尼安插在我们身边的唯一目的就是让曼尼来打探情报，监视我们，看我们有没有干坏事。

　　每次我和朋友聚会留宿都被曼尼搅局。上次罗利过来留宿是最悲惨的一次。

　　曼尼肯定是半夜有点冷，所以他爬进了罗利的睡袋来取暖。

　　这可把罗利给吓傻了，那次他早早就回家了。自那以后他就再没来我家过夜。

　　看来这次曼尼又要再把我和罗利的聚会留宿搅黄了。有曼尼在，我跟罗利就没法看恐怖片了，所以我们决定改为下棋。

　　我下棋下到有点想吐了，还有，罗利也快把我逼疯了。

　　他每隔5分钟就要去一趟洗手间，而且每次回来都要把枕头从房间的一边踢到另一边。

头几次还有点意思，但到后面多了就让我开始来气了。所以罗利又上楼去洗手间的时候，我整蛊了他一下。

　　我把老爸的一个哑铃放在枕头下面。果不其然，罗利再回来的时候又大踢了一脚。

　　很不幸，这回玩过火了。罗利哇哇大哭，像个大宝宝似的，我都没法让他安静下来。

　　罗利闹出这么大动静，老妈自然就下楼来了。

　　老妈看了看罗利的大拇趾，十分担忧。自从锡纸球事件之后，老妈对罗利在我们家里受伤的事就有些敏感，所以她直接开车送罗利回家了。

　　万幸的是老妈没有问我们事情的来龙去脉。

　　老妈和罗利一出门，我就知道，现在要赶紧做做曼尼的工作了。

　　曼尼看着我把哑铃搁在枕头下面，我知道他肯定会把我供出来的。所以我想出一个点子，让他不要打小报告。

　　我收拾了些行李，然后跟曼尼说因为我的所作所为，我无法面对老妈，只能离家出走，浪迹天涯了。

然后我走到门口，装得好像我真要一去不回似的。

我的这个点子是抄袭罗德里克的。那次他做了件什么坏事，知道我会揭发他，他就在我身上耍了这个把戏。他装成要离家出走，然后过了5分钟，他又回来了。

然而那一刻我已经准备好原谅他的一切了。

所以我跟曼尼说我要出走之后，就关上门，在外面等了个把分钟。当我开门的时候，我还指望看到他站在门廊大哭呢。结果曼尼压根不在那。我开始满屋子找他，猜猜我在哪儿找到他的？

就在地下室里，正在吃我的糖果。

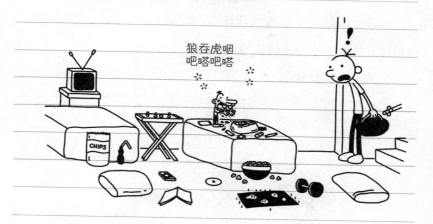

狼吞虎咽
吧嗒吧嗒

CHIPS

好吧，就当曼尼吃我的糖果是我为了让他保持缄默而必须付出的代价吧，这还是很划得来的。

星期六

早上醒来后，我下楼去厨房。一看老妈的脸色我就知道曼尼已经把我出卖了。

曼尼全都跟老妈说了。他连我们的恐怖片都说了。我都不知道他是怎么知道的，别问我。

老妈让我打电话给罗利道歉，然后又让我跟罗利的家长也道个歉。所以我下次被邀请去罗利家是遥遥无期了。

然后老妈拿起电话跟杰弗逊太太说话。杰弗逊太太说罗利的大拇趾骨折了，一周不能下地。

杰弗逊太太还说罗利"心都碎了"，因为他将不得不错过才艺秀的选拔赛了。他一整周都在跟斯科提·道格拉斯一起排练魔术。

所以老妈跟杰弗逊太太说我十分乐意来补罗利的缺参加选拔赛。我拼命地拉老妈的袖子，示意她这个点子糟透了，不过她自然是完全无视我的。

老妈挂电话之后，我跟她说打死我也不跟一个一年前还在穿纸尿裤的小·屁孩一起上台表演魔术。

但老妈无论如何不放过我，她还亲自把我押送到斯科提家跟他妈妈解释状况。现在看来是没有回头路了。

　　道格拉斯太太邀我进屋里，我跟斯科提上了他的房间，然后就开始排练。好啊，我发现的头一件令人震撼的事情就是，罗利跟斯科提在魔术表演中并不是平等的伙伴。罗利其实是斯科提的助手！

　　我跟斯科提说让我给一个小·学一年级学生当魔术师助手是绝对不可能的。不过斯科提说这是他的魔术道具，然后开始大哭大闹。

　　所以我只好乖乖地照斯科提的意思去做。说真的，我的麻烦已经够多的了。

斯科提递给我一件布满金光闪闪亮片的衬衫，他说这就是我的舞台服装。

这看起来就像奶奶去玩宾果游戏时穿的东西。我跟斯科提说我可以穿一些酷一点的衣服，比如皮夹克，不过他说那样会显得不够"魔幻"。

总而言之，其实在魔术表演中我所要做的就只是时不时给斯科提递一个道具，所以其实也不算太糟糕。

不过如果我们入围了，换作台下观众有500人，而不仅仅是斯科提含着奶嘴的妹妹的话，又另当别论了。所以，到时候你再问问我是什么感受吧。

星期天

我来跟你说说我跟斯科提·道格拉斯排练魔术表演之后的一大好处吧：它给了我很多灵感让我继续画漫画《呆子克雷登》。

罗利几个月前就不再为校报画连环画《祖维妈妈》了，因为他想多点时间来玩他的荧光恐龙玩具。这就意味着漫画撰稿人一职又空缺了，或许我可以试一试。

60

星期一

呃，关于才艺秀有一则喜讯。今天就是选拔赛，我跟斯科提没有入围。

好吧，作为一个助手，我或许本可以表现得更好的。但我可不是故意搞砸的。我只是偶尔忘记给他递道具罢了。

　　我们是唯一一队没有晋级的，说来还真有点难为情。

　　我知道我们不是今天选拔赛中表现最优秀的，但我们也不是最差劲的啊。有好些表演比我们的魔术表演还要蹩脚得多。

　　一个叫哈利·吉尔伯特森的幼儿园小·屁孩晋级了，而他的全部表演内容就是围着一台扬声器踩着轮滑绕"8"字圈罢了。扬声器播的还是《扬基曲①》。

　　罗德里克的乐队也晋级了，他还表现得好像取得了多大成就似的。

　　就像我之前所说的，罗德里克确实为冬季才艺秀兴奋不已。事实上他还提前一天完成了科学展的项目以便挤出时间好让乐队

　　① 《扬基曲》是一首广为流传的英文儿歌。

在大日子来临前多排练几次。

不过当罗德里克提交他的科学展项目的时候，他的科学老师跟他说他得从头来过，还要再想个别的点子。因为罗德里克完全没有运用假设前提、推理结论等"科学方法"来做他的项目。

罗德里克跟老师说，在他的"零重力"实验期间他真的长高了十六分之一英寸①，这就足以证明他这套还是有点道理的。

不过老师说这只是正常现象，每个像罗德里克这么大的男孩一个月都能长那么高。

唉，这对我来说可糟透的，因为我还打算将来做科学展也做"零重力"项目呢。

现在看来我所做的一切研究都是白费时间了。

① 1英寸等于2.54厘米。

老爸跟罗德里克说他得中断才艺秀以便开始新的实验，不过罗德里克说他可不打算这么干。

罗德里克跟老爸说他已经不再关心学校的事了。他说他的计划是在才艺秀上胜出，然后凭借演出的录影带跟唱片公司签约。然后他就退学，全职搞乐队，开始他的演艺生涯。

这个点子在我听来糟糕透了，不过老爸还是蛮开明的。

星期三

今晚就是冬季才艺秀的决赛了。我不大想去，老爸也是。不过老妈把我们都搞去了，说是去给罗德里克撑场。

罗德里克跟老妈提前去了学校，把乐队的东西先搬过去，所以老爸只能跟比尔开乐队的小货车了。老爸在学校停车场遇到公司上司的时候居然还神情自若。

　　大赛晚上7:00开始，我就直说吧，三校合办这个主意真是糟透了。

　　他们最后搞成这样：幼儿园小孩对着泰迪熊唱歌，后面跟的节目居然是18岁青年技巧速弹派金属吉他独奏。

我看老爸不太能接受拉利·拉金以及他穿的众多耳洞。拉利的吉他独奏到一半时，老爸靠过去跟旁边的人小小声说了话。

　　我想提醒老爸那人就是拉利的爸爸，但他没给我说话的机会。

　　三校合办才艺选秀的另一个问题就是有太多表演了，节目没完没了的。

　　到了9:30，他们决定一次上两个节目，好让晚会接着往下走。这个办法有时行得通，比如帕蒂·法瑞儿跳踢踏舞的时候，斯宾塞·吉特变戏法；不过其他时候，比如泰伦斯·詹姆斯骑着独轮车吹口琴的时候，查理丝·克莱朗诵她写的关于气候变暖的诗，这个效果就不敢恭维了。

罗德里克的乐队是最后一个上台的。

表演开始前，罗德里克让我给他们乐队录像，我跟他说我不干。

他最近对我这么恶劣，真不敢想象他这会儿居然还好意思找我帮忙。老妈自告奋勇负责拍摄。

罗德里克的乐队最后跟哈利·吉尔伯特森凑了一对。我确信罗德里克对此不太满意。

我发现罗德里克的乐队表演时，老爸没坐在我旁边，所以我四处张望，看他跑哪儿了。

老爸站在体育馆的后面，耳朵里塞着的棉球都凸出来了。老爸一直呆在那儿等乐队把歌唱完。

　　　乐队表演结束后，就开始颁奖了。罗德里克的乐队什么奖都没有拿到，倒是哈利·吉尔伯特森捧走了"最佳音乐艺术奖"。

不过你绝对猜不到，大奖的得主竟然是：罗利的保姆——勒兰德。

　　他凭借布偶戏胜出，因为评委认为他的节目"很有教益"。

　　我从不认为我跟罗德里克会在任何地方达成共识，但我不禁这样想：或许他说勒兰德是呆子还是有道理的。

　　晚会结束后，罗德里克的乐队到我们家来一起看演出录像。

　　他们一路满腹牢骚说他们上当了，还说什么评委对摇滚一窍不通。

　　所以他们打算直接把录像带寄去唱片公司，让录像带说话。

　　他们都在电视前坐好后，罗德里克把带子放进机子。不过，大概过了30秒大家就意识到这盘录像带一点价值都没有。

　　还记得罗德里克让老妈来给表演录像的事么？嗯，她拍得挺不错，只是前两分钟里她一直絮絮叨叨，没有停过。她的每一句品头论足都被摄像机录下了。

每次比尔像摇滚明星一样伸出舌头上下抖动时，你就会听到老妈开始发议论了。

事实上，老妈唯一停嘴的时候就是罗德里克表演爵士鼓独奏的时候。不过那时候摄像机抖得太厉害了，根本什么都看不清。

一开始，罗德里克跟他的队友都气坏了。不过忽然有人想起学校也全程录像了，应该是明晚在本地有线频道上播出。

　　我猜这就是说他们会全体再回来看那个的。

星期四

　　唉，刚才几个小·时真是受罪极了。

　　罗德里克和他的队友晚上7:00就来看才艺秀了。他们全程坐在那里，三个小·时没换过台，直到他们的乐队上场。

　　学校做了件好事，演出录像拍得不错，一切看来都挺好，直到罗德里克开始爵士鼓独奏。

　　就是那时候老妈开始跳舞的。然后那个不知何方神圣的摄像师就开始对着老妈给特写了，摄像机就这么一直对着老妈，直到全曲结束。

　　也就是说罗德里克没有任何东西可以寄给唱片公司。他为此大发雷霆。

一开始他很生老妈的气，以为她把事情搞得一团糟。不过老妈说如果罗德里克不想让人跳舞，那他就不该放音乐。

然后罗德里克把矛头转向我。他说这全是我的错，如果我当初乖乖听话去帮他拍录像的话，事情就不会落到这个地步。

但我跟他说要不是他这么可恶的话，我会帮他拍的。

然后我们就开始互骂。老爸和老妈把我们分开，然后把罗德里克带回他楼下的房间，把我送回我的房间。

几小时后我下楼去，刚好在厨房碰见罗德里克。他面带微笑，我知道肯定出事了。

罗德里克跟我说我的秘密已经走漏风声了。

一开始我还没搞清楚他指的是什么。过了半晌才明白过来，他说的是今年夏天的那件事。

我跑到地下室，拿起罗德里克的手机看看他有没有给谁打过电话。果不其然，他基本上把每个朋友的电话都打了一遍，而且还是那些有着跟我同龄的弟弟妹妹的朋友。

到了明早，学校里就人人都知道那件事了。而且我敢保证罗德里克肯定添油加醋，让故事听起来更加不堪入耳了。

既然秘密已经泄露了，那我就公开真相，录以备案吧，可不是罗德里克的歪曲版本哦。

那我就开始说了。

今年夏天，我跟罗德里克不得不跟爷爷在他的"休闲塔"公寓里住几天。但在那里完全无事可做，我无聊得快发疯了。

百无聊赖之际，我就掏出我的老日志，开始写写画画。不过当着罗德里克的面拿出一本封面写着"日记"的本子来实在是犯了一个致命的错误。

罗德里克抢走我的日志，拔腿就跑。要不是因为"勇者无惧"的棋盘还摊了一地，他或许就已经冲进洗手间把门锁起来了。

我从地上抓起日志本就往外跑，跑到走廊，冲下楼梯，然后躲进大堂的一个洗手间，把自己锁在一个隔间里。

　　我把双脚抬离地面，这样如果罗德里克追进来，他也不会发现我在这里。

　　我深知如果我的日志落到罗德里克手里，那我的噩梦就开始了。所以我决定把整本日志撕成碎片，然后冲进马桶。宁可毁掉它，也不能让它落入罗德里克之手。

撕扯

　　我刚开始撕书就听见洗手间的门开了，我以为是罗德里克，所以屏住呼吸，动也不动。

　　接下来我又什么动静都没听到，所以我从隔间的上面往外面窥探一下情况。就在这时，我看到一个女人在镜子前面化妆。

我以为是那女人不小心进了男厕，因为"休闲塔"里的人们经常这样。

　　我刚想开口说话告诉这位女士她进错洗手间了，刚好又有一个人进来了。猜猜怎么着？是另一个女人。

　　这时候我才意识到我才是那个不速之客，是我进了女厕。

　　我暗暗祈祷，盼望这些女人赶紧洗完手就走，这样我就能赶紧逃离是非之地。不过她们在我两旁的隔间坐下来了。而且每次一个女人走出洗手间又会有另一个女人进来。所以我根本没机会跑出去。

　　要是罗利觉得自己被迫吞了千年奶酪①是遭了大罪的话，他真该来尝尝在"休闲塔"女厕被困一个半小时的滋味。

　　我猜是终于有人听到了我的动静，然后到前台举报了我。几分钟后，整栋楼就传遍了这个消息：女厕所里有"色狼"。

　　① "千年奶酪"详见《小屁孩日记②》。

75

　　等到保安进来把我逮出去的时候，"休闲塔"的每一个住户都已经来到大堂了。而且罗德里克在爷爷的电视机上目睹了全过程。

　　既然事已败露，我知道自己是没脸回学校了。所以我跟老妈说，我非转学不可了，而且我还把原因跟她交代了。

　　老妈说我不该为别人的想法而苦恼。我只是犯了一个"无心之失"，大家会理解的。

　　这就彻底地证明了老妈完全不了解我们这个年龄的小孩。

　　现在我又因为没有跟马马杜保持书信来往而自责了。因为如

76

果我跟他还保持联系的话，说不定我还能去法国做交换生，在那里避几年风头呢。

我只知道，我明天唯一不想去的地方就是学校，但那似乎恰是我唯一能去的地方。

星期五

今天，最疯狂的事情发生了。我刚一踏进校门，就被一群家伙围住了，我做好心理准备，等着他们开始取笑我。不过他们并没有骚扰我，反而开始祝贺我。

① 〈法〉"你好吗？"

人人都来跟我握手、拍拍我的后背，我都搞不懂这是怎么回事。

　　大家七嘴八舌都在跟我说话，我费了好一阵子才听出点所以然。不过一定是这么回事：

　　罗德里克把故事跟朋友们说了，朋友们又把故事讲给自己的弟弟妹妹，然后弟弟妹妹又跟他们的朋友八卦了。

　　等到流言四起时，一切细节都完全变样了。

　　故事就从我误入"休闲塔"女厕所讹传为我潜入克罗斯兰高中的女更衣室了。

　　我不敢相信整件事情居然扭曲成这样，但我也不打算澄清了。

忽然之间，我成了学校的英雄人物。我还得了个绰号。人们管我叫"潜行侠"。

　　而且居然有人给我做了一条"潜行侠"头巾，那我肯定戴啦。这种好事从未在我身上降临过，我自然不会拒绝我的光荣时刻。

　　破天荒第一次，我尝到了成为全校最红红人的滋味。

　　不幸的是，我在女生中就相对没有那么吃香了。实情是，或许我连找个女生跟我一起去情人节舞会都没指望了。

　　还记得罗德里克多么希望自己的乐队受人关注么？好吧，他的愿望实现了，因为现在人人都知道水不湿是谁了。

　　我猜一定是有人觉得老妈在才艺秀上手舞足蹈的录像十分有趣，因为现在网上到处是这段视频。现在人人都知道罗德里克·赫夫利是"跳舞老妈"视频中的鼓手了。

　　从那以后，罗德里克就一直躲在地下室里，等着事件平息下去。我不得不承认，我还真有点为他感到难过。

　　我也因学校那段视频而被讥笑，不过至少我没在视频中露脸啊。

　　尽管罗德里克有时候挺可恶的，但好歹他是我哥哥啊。

　　明天就是科学展了，如果罗德里克没法交差的话，他就要被学校扫地出门了。

　　因此我才对他施以援手，不过仅此一次下不为例。我们整晚一起赶工，不是我吹牛，我们还真干得不错。

无论如何，当罗德里克明天拿到头奖，科学课顺利过关的时候，我只希望他知道自己有多么走运，因为有我这么一个弟弟。

致 谢

对于我的家人，我永远满怀感激，因为他们给我提供了我创作所需的灵感、鼓励与支持。我要好好感谢我的兄弟斯科特和帕特、我的姐姐莱，还有我的父母亲。没有你们就不会有赫夫利一家。谢谢我的太太牛莉和我的孩子们，他们为我圆梦漫画家而做出了太多牺牲。我也要谢谢我的岳父岳母，汤姆和吉儿，在我每次截稿前后他们都陪伴左右，帮前帮后。

感谢阿布拉姆斯出版集团的一干好汉，尤其是查理·科赫曼，一个极敬业的编辑，一个大好人，感谢我有幸与之一同亲密合作的阿布拉姆斯出版同仁：詹森·威尔斯、霍华德·李维斯、苏珊·梵·米特、查德·贝克曼、萨马拉·克莱、瓦莱里·拉尔夫和斯科特·奥尔巴赫。尤其要向米歇尔·雅各布致以谢意。

感谢杰斯·布莱利尔把格雷·赫夫利带向全世界。感谢贝琦·比尔德，多谢她发挥她相当的影响力来四处宣传《小屁孩日记》。最后，感谢迪·斯科尔-弗莱，以及全国所有书商，谢谢你们把这些书送到孩子们手里。

作者简介

杰夫·金尼，Poptropica.com的创始人，《纽约时报》畅销榜第一畅销书《小屁孩日记》的作者。他在华盛顿度过童年，1995

年移居新英格兰州。杰夫现与妻子朱莉、两个儿子威尔和格兰特居住在南马萨诸塞州。

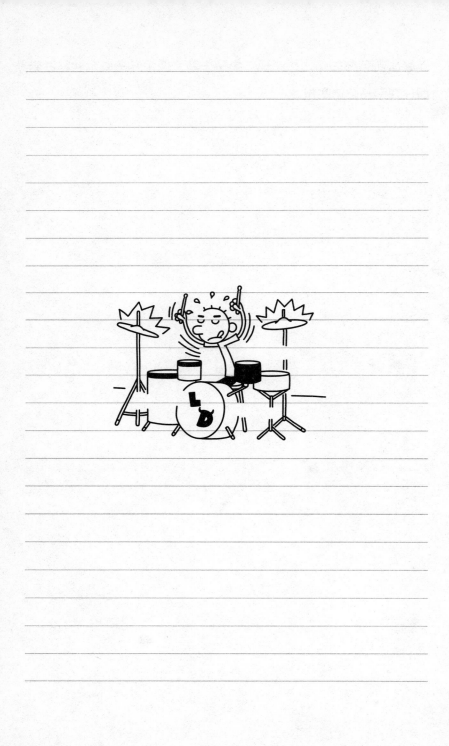

TO JULIE, WILL, AND GRANT

The Hefflys

Granda   Dad   Mom   Manny   Rowley

DIARY
of a
Wimpy Kid

by Jeff Kinney

Rodrick

Gregory

NOVEMBER

<u>Monday</u>

It's been over a week since Rodrick's party, and I stopped worrying that Mom and Dad were gonna bust us for it. But remember that bathroom door we switched out? Well, I forgot all about it until tonight.

Rodrick was upstairs in my room bugging me, and Dad went into the bathroom. A couple seconds later, he said something that made Rodrick stop cold.

HEY...DIDN'T THIS DOOR USED TO LOCK?

I thought it was over. If Dad knew about the DOOR, it was just a matter of time before he found out about the party.

But Dad didn't put two and two together.

You know, maybe it wouldn't be so bad if Mom and Dad found out about the party. Rodrick would get grounded, which would be AWESOME. So if I can figure out a way to spill the beans without Rodrick finding out, I'm gonna go for it.

Tuesday

I got my first letter from my French pen pal, Mamadou, today. I decided to adjust my attitude and give this whole pen-pal thing my best effort. So when I wrote back to Mamadou today, I tried to be as helpful as possible.

Dear Gregory,
 I am very privileged
to make your acquaintance.
                    Mamadou

Dear Mamadou,

I'm pretty sure "aquaintance"
doesn't have a "c" in it.

I really think you need to work
on your English.

                    Sincerely, Greg

I think it's dumb that Madame Lefrere won't let
us use e-mail with our pen pals. Albert Murphy
has already written back and forth with his pen
pal a bunch of times, and it's costing them a lot
of money in stamps.

Dear Jacques—	Dear Albert,	Dear Jacques—
How old are you?	12.	Oh.

COST: $14

<u>Friday</u>

Tonight, Rowley's parents went out to dinner, so they got him a babysitter.

I don't know why Rowley can't just watch himself for a few hours, but believe me I'm not complaining. Rowley's babysitter is Heather Hills, and she's the prettiest girl at Crossland High School.

So whenever the Jeffersons go out, I always make sure to be up at Rowley's for "story time".

I went up to Rowley's at about 8:00 tonight. I even splashed on some of Rodrick's cologne to make sure I made a good impression on Heather.

I knocked on the door and waited for Heather
to answer. But I was caught a little off guard
when Rowley's next-door neighbor Leland
answered instead.

I can't believe Rowley's parents switched
babysitters from Heather to LELAND. They
should've at least checked with me before doing
something stupid like THAT.

Once I realized Heather wasn't there, I turned
around to go back home. But Rowley asked me if
I wanted to hang out and play Magick and
Monsters with him and Leland.

The only reason I said "yes" was because I thought it was some kind of video game. But then I found out that you play it with pencils and paper and these special dice, and that you're supposed to use your "imagination" or whatever.

It actually turned out to be pretty fun, mostly because in Magick and Monsters you can do all sorts of stuff you could never do in real life.

When I got home, I told Mom all about Magick and Monsters and how Leland was a really awesome Dungeon Keeper. Rodrick overheard me talking about Leland, and he said that Leland is the biggest nerd at his high school.

But this is coming from a guy who spends his Saturday nights putting fake throw-up on people's cars in the Home Depot parking lot. So I think I'll just take Rodrick's opinion with a grain of salt.

Wednesday

I've been going up to Leland's house every day after school to play Magick and Monsters. I was headed up there again today when Mom stopped me at the door.

Mom has been acting real suspicious of this whole Magick and Monsters thing.

And from the questions she's been asking me, I guess she must think Leland is teaching me and Rowley witchcraft or something. So today, Mom said she wanted to go WITH me to Leland's to watch us play.

I BEGGED Mom not to come, because first of all I knew she would never approve of all the violence in the game.

And second of all, I knew that having her in the room would totally ruin the whole experience for everyone.

When I begged Mom not to join us, it made her even MORE suspicious. So now there was no changing her mind.

Rowley and Leland couldn't have cared less that Mom came with me. But I couldn't enjoy myself, because I felt like a total dork playing in front of her.

UH...MY WIZARD TALROC UTTERS THE SPELL OF TALRUNE.

I figured Mom would eventually get bored and just go home, but she stuck around. And right when I thought she was finally gonna leave, Mom said that SHE wanted to join in the game.

So Leland started setting up a character for Mom, even though I was trying to signal to him that it was a big mistake.

When Leland created a character for Mom, Mom told Leland she wanted HER character to be MY character's mother in the game.

I did some quick thinking and told Mom that all the characters in Magick and Monsters are orphans, so she couldn't be my mother.

And Mom believed me. But then she asked Leland if she could NAME her character "Mom," and he said "yes".

I have to give Mom credit for figuring out that loophole, but it totally ruined the rest of the game for me.

Even though Mom wasn't technically my mother in the game, she sure ACTED like she was.

At this one point, our characters were hanging out in a tavern waiting for a spy to arrive, and my dwarf, Grimlon, ordered a pint of mead. Mead is sort of like beer in Magick and Monsters, and I guess Mom didn't approve of THAT.

MOM ACCIDENTALLY BUMPS GRIMLON'S ARM AND SPILLS HIS DRINK.

The worst part of the game was when we got into a battle situation. See, the whole point of Magick and Monsters is that you're supposed to kill as many monsters as possible so you can get points and move up in levels.

But I don't really think Mom got that concept.

After about an hour of things going like this, I decided to quit. So I gathered up my stuff, and me and Mom headed home.

On the way back, Mom was really talking up Magick and Monsters, saying how it could help me with my "math skills" and stuff like that. All I can say is, I hope she isn't planning on becoming a regular at these games. Because the first chance I get, "Mom" is getting handed over to a pack of Orcs.

Thursday
After school today, Mom took me to the bookstore and bought just about every Magick and Monsters book on the shelf. She must've dropped about $200, and she didn't even make me cash in a single Mom Buck.

I realized maybe I judged Mom a little too quick, and maybe it wasn't such a bad thing having her in our group after all.

I was all set to take my new books up to Leland's, but that's when I found out there was a catch.

Mom actually bought all those books so me and RODRICK could play Magick and Monsters together. She said it was a good way for the two of us to work out our differences.

Mom told Rodrick she wanted him to be the Dungeon Keeper, just like Leland. Then she dumped the pile of books on Rodrick's bed and told him to start studying up.

It was bad enough playing in front of Mom at Leland's house, but I knew playing with Rodrick would be about ten times worse.

Mom was serious about me and Rodrick playing together, so I knew I was gonna have to go through with it. I spent about an hour up in my room making up characters with names Rodrick couldn't make fun of, like "Joe" and "Bob".

Once I was finished, I met Rodrick in the kitchen, and we started our game.

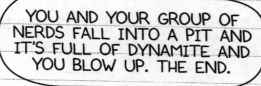

YOU AND YOUR GROUP OF NERDS FALL INTO A PIT AND IT'S FULL OF DYNAMITE AND YOU BLOW UP. THE END.

I guess I should be grateful that it was over with quickly. And I just hope Mom saved her receipts on those books.

Friday

The teachers have really been cracking down on kids copying off of each other this year. Remember how I said I was glad I got put next to Alex Aruda in Pre-Algebra? Well, THAT hasn't done me any good.

Mrs. Lee is my Pre-Algebra teacher, and I'm guessing she also had Rodrick when he was in middle school. Because that woman watches me like a HAWK.

Sometimes I think it would be really cool if I had a glass eye or something like that. First of all, I could use it to play all sorts of wacky tricks on my friends.

HERE, CATCH!

OK! WHAT IS IT?

But the main thing I'd use it for is to help me get better grades.

104

On the first day of school, I'd aim my glass eye down like this:

Then I'd go up to the teacher and say, "Listen, I just wanted to tell you I have a glass eye. So don't go thinking I'm looking at other people's papers."

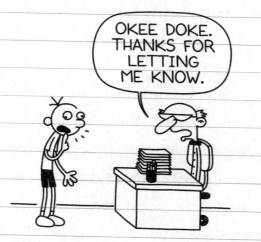

Then, during a test, I'd aim my glass eye down at my OWN paper, and I'd look at some brainy kid's paper with my REAL eye.

I could copy away! And the teacher would be too dumb to notice.

THAT POOR GLASS EYE KID.

Unfortunately, I DON'T have a glass eye. So if Mom asks me why I flunked my pop quiz in Pre-Algebra today, that's my excuse.

Sunday
Rodrick has been hitting Mom and Dad up for cash lately, so I guess the Mom Bucks program isn't really working out for him. Mom has tried to make Rodrick do more chores to earn some money, but that hasn't been going too well.

IS THIS HOW YOU DO IT?

YOU NEED TO BE USING A CLEAN RAG, SON!

But tonight, Mom figured out a way Rodrick could earn some cash. My school sent home a newsletter saying that Music Education has been cancelled because of budget cuts, so parents should get their kids private music lessons.

Mom told Rodrick he could give ME private drum lessons, and that she would PAY him for it.

I think Mom came up with the idea because lately Rodrick's been telling everyone he's a "professional drummer".

There's this local show called the "Community Follies" where all the neighborhood parents do a bunch of comedy skits, and it's been running in our local theater for about two weeks.

The other night, the regular drummer got sick, so Rodrick filled in, and he got paid five bucks.

I don't know if that really makes Rodrick a "professional drummer", but that didn't stop me from using it to score points with the girls at school.

When Mom told Rodrick he should start giving me drum lessons, he wasn't too hot on the idea. But then Mom said she'd pay him ten dollars a lesson, and that I could get a bunch of my friends to sign up, too.

So now I've gotta recruit some people for Rodrick's Drum Academy. And I can already tell, this isn't gonna be a lot of fun.

Monday
I couldn't get any of my friends to sign up for Rodrick's drum school except Rowley, and I kind of had to trick HIM into doing it. Rowley is always saying he wants to learn how to play the drums, but he wants to play the kind they use in marching bands.

I told Rowley I knew for a FACT that Rodrick was going to cover all that stuff in week four, and that got Rowley pretty excited.

I was just glad I wasn't gonna have to take drum lessons all by myself.

Rowley came over after school, and we went down to the basement to start our first lesson. Rodrick started us off with some pretty basic drum drills.

There was only one practice pad and two drum-sticks, so Rowley had to use a paper plate and some plastic utensils. But I guess that's what happens when you're the last person to sign up for a class.

TAPPITY TAP

TAP DOINK

After about fifteen minutes, Rodrick got a call from
Ward, and that put an end to our first lesson.

Mom wasn't too happy to see me and Rowley
upstairs so soon, and she sent us back down to
the basement. She said not to come up until
Rodrick had at least given us a practice assignment.
So he did.

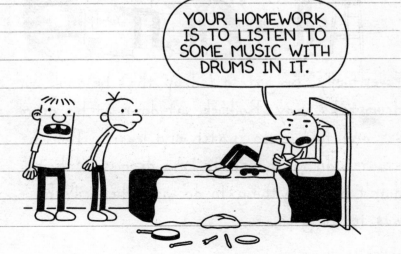

Tuesday
Me and Rowley had drum lessons with Rodrick
again today.

Well, Rodrick might be a good drummer, but he's
not a good teacher. Me and Rowley tried our best
to do the drills Rodrick taught us, but every time
we messed up, Rodrick would get frustrated.

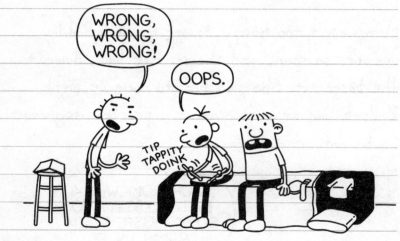

Eventually, he got so fed up that he took our
drumsticks away. Rodrick sat down at his drum
set and told us to "watch and learn". Then he
started doing this really long drum solo that
didn't have anything to do with the drills he
was teaching us.

Rodrick didn't even look up from his drum set when me and Rowley left and went upstairs.

I'm not complaining, though. Because the way I see it, this way everyone wins.

Thursday
We've got a History paper due the day before Thanksgiving, and I'd better start getting serious about it.

The teachers are getting a lot stricter about the quality of work we turn in, and the way I usually do things isn't working so good anymore.

Last week we had a paper due in Science, and Mrs. Breckman said we had to choose an animal to write about. So I picked the moose. I know I should have gone to the library and done research, but I just decided to wing it.

The Amazing Moose
by Greg Heffley

Diet: The moose eats many, many things, but the list would be way too long to put in this paper. So I will save us all some time by just listing the things that the moose does NOT eat.

BUBBLE GUM   METAL   PIZZA

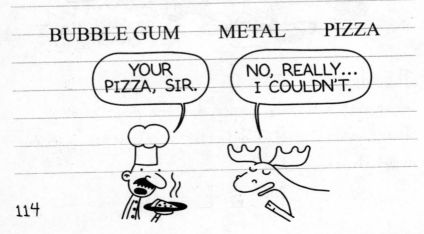

Even though there are moose habitats set up all over the place, the moose is almost extinct.

Everybody knows the moose evolved from birds, just like people did. But somewhere along the line people got arms, and the moose got stuck with those useless horns.

THE END

I actually thought I did a pretty good job. But I guess Mrs. Breckman must be an expert on mooses or something, because she made me go to the library and start the paper over from scratch.

And my NEXT paper isn't gonna be any easier. I have to write a poem about the 1900s for Mr. Huff's class, and I don't know the first thing about History OR poetry. So I guess I'd better start hitting the books.

Monday
I was up at Rowley's playing board games yesterday, and the craziest thing happened. When Rowley was in the bathroom, I noticed that there was some play money sticking out of the box of one of the other games.

I couldn't believe my eyes. Because the play money inside that game was the EXACT same kind of money Mom uses for Mom Bucks.

When I counted it up, there was something like $100,000 in cash in that box.

It only took me about two seconds to figure out what to do next.

When I got home, I ran upstairs and stuffed the money under my mattress. I tossed and turned all night trying to figure out what to do with my new Mom Bucks.

I realized Mom would probably have some way of knowing the difference between phony Mom Bucks and the real thing. So this morning, I decided to try a little experiment.

I asked Mom if I could cash in some Mom Bucks so I could buy stamps to write to my pen pal. I was really nervous when I handed Mom the money.

But she took it without even blinking.

I can't believe my luck! I figure I can make this $100,000 last all the way through high school, and maybe even farther. I might not even have to get a real job later on.

The trick will be to not cash in too much at one time, or Mom will know something's up.

And I have to remember to earn a few Mom Bucks for real here and there so she doesn't get too suspicious.

I will say one thing for sure, though, and it's that I won't be using the money Mom gave me to buy stamps.

I got a picture from my pen-pal, Mamadou, in the mail yesterday, and that pretty much killed any chance of me writing HIM back.

<u>Tuesday</u>

My big History paper is due tomorrow, but they've been saying all week that it's gonna snow about a FOOT tonight.

So I haven't really been sweating it all that much.

At around 10:00, I peeked out the window to see how many inches of snow were on the ground so far. But I couldn't believe my eyes when I pulled back the curtain.

Man, I was counting on school being CANCELLED tomorrow. I turned on the news to see what happened, but the weather guy was telling a TOTALLY different story than he was three hours ago.

WE REALLY DODGED A BULLET THIS TIME, BOB!

YOU CAN SAY THAT AGAIN, BARBARA! HA HA HA!

That meant I had to get cracking on my History paper. The problem was, it was too late to go to the library, and we don't have any books in our house that are about the 1900s. So I knew I had to think of something quick.

Then I had a great idea.

Dad has bailed Rodrick out a MILLION times on his school papers. So I figured he could help me, too.

I told Dad about my situation, thinking he'd jump right in and help. But I guess Dad has learned his lesson in that department.

GOOD LUCK WITH THAT!

Rodrick must have overheard me talking to Dad, because he told me I should follow him downstairs.

You know how Rodrick had Mr. Huff, my History teacher, in middle school? Well, it turns out Mr. Huff gave Rodrick's class the EXACT same assignment when he was in my grade.

Rodrick dug around in his junk drawer and found his old paper. And then he told me he'd sell it to me for five bucks.

I told him there was no WAY I'd do that.

I'll admit, it was pretty tempting. Because number one, since all of Rodrick's assignments have gone through Dad, I knew Rodrick got a good grade on his paper. And number two, it was in one of those clear plastic binders that teachers go crazy for.

Plus, I had a huge stash of Mom Bucks under my mattress upstairs, and I knew I could pay Rodrick with that.

But I couldn't do it. I mean, I've copied off of people's papers on quizzes and stuff before, but BUYING a paper off of someone would be taking it to a whole nother level.

So I decided I was gonna just have to suck it up and do the paper myself.

I started doing some research on the computer, but at about midnight, the worst possible thing happened: The power went out.

That's when I knew I was in some serious trouble. I knew I'd flunk History if I didn't turn in a paper. So even though I didn't want to, I decided to take Rodrick up on his offer.

I scraped together $500 in Mom Bucks and
went down to the basement. But Rodrick didn't
let me off that easy.

Rodrick told me his new price was $20,000 in
Mom Bucks. I told him I didn't have it, so he
just rolled over and went back to sleep.

At that point, I was really desperate. So I
went upstairs and grabbed a big handful of
thousand dollar bills and brought them down to
Rodrick's room. I gave him the money, and he
turned over the paper. I felt really bad about
what I did, but I just tried not to think
about it and went to sleep.

<u>Wednesday</u>
On the bus ride to school, I took Rodrick's paper
out of my bag. But I took one look at it and
knew something was seriously wrong.

First of all, the poem wasn't typed out. It was
in Rodrick's own handwriting.

That's when it hit me: Dad only started doing
Rodrick's papers for him once he got to HIGH
school. So that meant this paper was Rodrick's
OWN work.

I started reading Rodrick's paper to see if I
could still use it. But apparently, Rodrick was
even worse about doing his research than ME.

126

A Hundred Years Ago
by Rodrick Heffley

Sometimes I sit and wonder
About stuff I don't know
Like what the heck the earth was like
A hundred years ago.

Did cavemen ride on dinosaurs?
Did flowers even grow?
Well we could guess but that was back
A hundred years ago.

I wish they built a time machine
And they picked me to go
To check out what the scene was like
A hundred years ago.

Did giant spiders rule the earth?
Were deserts filled with snow?
I wonder what the story was
A hundred years ago.

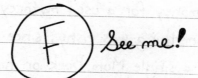

F See me!

I guess I learned my lesson about buying a paper off someone. Or at least off of RODRICK.

When third period rolled around, I didn't have anything to turn in to Mr. Huff. I guess that means I'll be taking summer school for History.

And my day got a whole lot worse after that. When I got home from school, Mom was waiting for me at the front door.

You know that stack of bills I paid Rodrick with? Well, he tried to cash them ALL in at once to get money for a used motorcycle. I'm sure Mom knew something was fishy, since Rodrick has never earned a single Mom Buck on his own.

128

Rodrick told Mom where he got the money, and she dug around my room until she found my stash under the mattress. Mom knew she never put $100,000 into circulation, so she confiscated ALL my cash, even the ones I earned for real. I guess that's the end of the Mom Bucks program.

To be honest with you, I'm kind of relieved. Sleeping on that pile of cash every night was really stressing me out.

Mom was mad that I tried to put one over on her like that, so she gave me a punishment. But I got that out of the way before dinner.

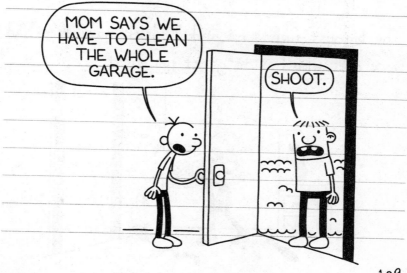

MOM SAYS WE HAVE TO CLEAN THE WHOLE GARAGE.

SHOOT.

<u>Thursday</u>
Today was Thanksgiving, and it started off like
it always does: with Aunt Loretta showing up
two hours early.

Mom always makes me and Rodrick "entertain"
Aunt Loretta, and that means talk to her until
the rest of the family shows up.

The biggest fights me and Rodrick have ever had
were over who has to greet her first.

The rest of the family started trickling in around 11:00. Dad's brother, Uncle Joe, and his kids were the last ones to show up around 12:30.

Uncle Joe's kids all call Dad the same thing.

HI AUNT FWANK!

Mom thinks it's really cute, but Dad swears that Uncle Joe tells his kids to do it on purpose.

Things are pretty tense between Dad and Uncle Joe, because Dad is still mad at Uncle Joe for something he did LAST Thanksgiving. Back then, Manny had just started potty training, and he was doing pretty good. In fact, he was probably about two weeks from being out of diapers.

But Uncle Joe said something to Manny that changed everything.

BETTER LOOK OUT FOR THE "POTTY MONSTER", LITTLE FELLA!

It was six months before Manny would even step foot in the bathroom again.

Every time Dad changed a dirty diaper after that, I heard him cursing Uncle Joe under his breath.

We had dinner around 2:00, and then people went into the living room to talk. I didn't feel like talking, so I went in the family room to play video games.

Eventually, I guess Dad had enough of the family, too, so he went downstairs to work on his Civil War battlefield. But he forgot to lock the door to the furnace room, and Uncle Joe walked in after him.

Uncle Joe seemed pretty interested in what Dad was working on, so Dad told him all about it.

Dad gave Uncle Joe this big speech about the 150th Regiment and the role it played at Gettysburg, and spent about a half hour describing the whole battle.

But I don't think Uncle Joe was really listening to Dad's speech.

NICE TOYS, BIG BROTHER!

Thanksgiving didn't last too much longer after that. Dad went upstairs and turned up the thermostat until it got stuffy and everyone cleared out. And that's pretty much how Thanksgiving ends every year at our house.

DECEMBER

Saturday

You remember how I said Mom and Dad were going to eventually find out about Rodrick's party? Well, it finally happened today.

Mom sent Dad out to pick up the pictures from Thanksgiving, and when Dad got back, you could tell he wasn't happy about something.

The picture in Dad's hand was from Rodrick's party.

It looked like one of Rodrick's friends accidentally took a picture with Mom's camera, which she keeps on the shelf above the stereo. And when he took the picture, it captured the whole scene.

Rodrick tried to deny that he had a party. But everything was right there in the picture, so there really wasn't any point.

Mom and Dad took away Rodrick's car keys and told him his punishment is that he's not allowed to leave the house for a whole MONTH.

They were even mad at ME, because they said I was Rodrick's "accomplice". So I got hit with a two-week video game ban.

Sunday

Mom and Dad have been all over Rodrick's case ever since they found out about his party. Rodrick usually sleeps until 2:00 in the afternoon on weekends, but today Dad made Rodrick get out of bed by 8:00 A.M.

Making Rodrick get out of bed early is a pretty big blow to him, because Rodrick LOVES to sleep. One time last fall, Rodrick slept for thirty-six hours STRAIGHT.

He slept all the way from Sunday night until Tuesday morning, and he didn't even realize he missed a whole day of his life until Tuesday night.

But it looks like Rodrick has found a way around the new 8:00 rule. Now, when Dad tells Rodrick to get out of bed, Rodrick just drags his stuff upstairs with him and he sleeps on the couch until it's time for dinner. So I guess you gotta give this round to Rodrick.

<u>Tuesday</u>
Mom and Dad are going away again this weekend, and they're dropping me and Rodrick off at Grandpa's. They said they WERE gonna let us stay home, but we proved we can't be trusted on our own.

Grandpa lives over in Leisure Towers, which is this old folks' home. I had to spend a week there with Rodrick a few months ago, and it was the low point of my whole summer.

Manny is staying with Gramma this weekend, and I'd give ANYTHING to trade places with him. Gramma always has her fridge stocked with soda and cake and stuff like that, and she has cable TV with all the movie channels.

The reason Manny is going to Gramma's is because Manny is Gramma's favorite. And all you need to do is take one look at her refrigerator for the proof.

But if anyone ever accuses Gramma of showing favorites, she gets all defensive.

And it's not just the pictures on the fridge, either. Gramma has Manny's drawings and stuff hanging up all over the house.

The only thing that Gramma has from ME is this note I wrote her when I was six. I was mad at her because she wouldn't give me any ice cream before dinner, so here's what I wrote:

I hate you Gram-ma

Gramma has kept that note all these years, and she's STILL holding it over my head.

AND THIS IS WHAT MY WONDERFUL GRANDSON GREGORY MADE FOR ME!

I guess every grandparent has their favorite, and I can understand that. But at least Grandpa is up front about it.

<u>Saturday</u>

Well, Mom and Dad dumped me and Rodrick off at Grandpa's today, just like they said they were gonna do.

I started looking for ways to entertain myself, but there's nothing in Grandpa's condo that's fun to do, so I just sat down with him and watched TV. But Grandpa doesn't even watch real shows. He just keeps his TV tuned to the security camera that's in the front lobby of his building.

And after a few hours of THAT, you start to go a little nuts.

OH, SURE! BARRY GROSSMAN HAS TIME TO GO OUT FOR A THREE-HOUR WALK, BUT HE DOESN'T HAVE TIME TO RETURN MY VACUUM!

At about 5:00, Grandpa made us dinner. Grandpa makes this awful thing called "watercress salad", and it's the worst thing you ever tasted.

It's basically a bunch of cold green beans and cucumbers floating in a pool of vinegar.

Rodrick knows I hate watercress salad more than ANYTHING, so the last time we stayed at Grandpa's, Rodrick made sure to pile it on my plate.

I had to sit there and choke down every bite so Grandpa's feelings wouldn't be hurt.

And guess what I got as a reward for cleaning my plate?

Tonight, Grandpa gave us our salad, and I acted like I was gonna eat it. But then I just stuffed it all in my pocket when no one was looking.

It felt pretty disgusting when the cold vinegar started running down my leg, but believe me it was about a thousand times better than having to EAT it.

After dinner, the three of us went into the living room. Grandpa has all these really old board games, and he always makes me and Rodrick play them with him.

He has this one game called "Gutbusters", where one player reads a card, and the other player tries not to laugh.

144

I always beat Grandpa, mostly because the jokes don't make any sense to me.

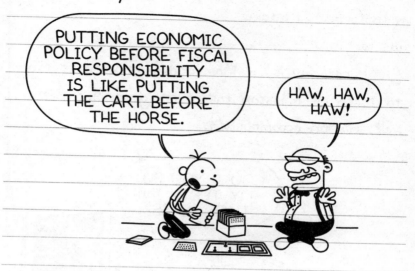

I always beat Rodrick, too, but that's because Rodrick loses on purpose. Whenever it's my turn to read a card, he makes sure he has a big mouthful of milk.

At 10:00, I was ready for bed. But Rodrick called the couch, and that meant I had to sleep with Grandpa again.

All I can say is, if Mom and Dad were trying to teach me a lesson for covering for Rodrick, well, mission accomplished.

COULD YOU PUT MY TEETH IN THAT GLASS?

Sunday

Rodrick has a big Science Fair project due right before Christmas break, and it looks like Mom and Dad are making Rodrick do this one all by himself.

Last year, Rodrick's science project was called "Does Watching Violent Movies Make People Think Violent Thoughts?".

I guess the idea was to have people watch horror movies and then draw pictures afterward to show how the movies affected them.

But it was really just an excuse for Rodrick and his friends to watch a bunch of horror movies on school nights.

Rodrick's friends got the movie-watching part done, but they didn't draw a single picture. And the night before the Science Fair, Rodrick didn't have anything to show for himself.

So me, Mom, and Dad had to bail Rodrick out. Dad typed up the paper, Mom made the poster board stuff, and I had to draw a bunch of pictures.

I did my best to imagine what teenagers would draw after watching violent movies.

The thing that REALLY stinks is that I caught heat from Mom when she saw my drawings, because she said they were "disturbing". And that's why I was only allowed to watch G-rated movies for the rest of the year.

But if you want to talk about "disturbing", you should've seen some of the stuff Manny was coming up with those days.

One night, Rodrick accidentally left one of his horror movies in the DVD player, and when Manny went to turn on cartoons the next day, he got Rodrick's movie instead.

I came across a couple of Manny's drawings after that, and some of them were enough to give ME nightmares.

<u>Tuesday</u>

Mom and Dad set up due dates for Rodrick on his Science Fair project, and by 6:00 tonight, he was supposed to tell them the theme of his experiment.

But at 6:45, things weren't looking so good.

Rodrick was watching a show about astronauts, and what happens to them after they've been up in space for a long time. The show said that when the astronauts get back to Earth, they're actually TALLER than when they left.

And the reason is because there's no gravity in space, so their spines decompress or something.

Well, that gave Rodrick the idea he was looking for.

Rodrick told Mom and Dad he was going to do his science experiment on the effect of "zero gravity" on the human spine. And from the way Rodrick was talking it up, you'd think the results of his experiment were gonna benefit mankind.

Dad seemed pretty impressed. Or maybe he was just relieved that Rodrick actually came through on his first task. But I think Dad started to see things a little different later on when he told Rodrick to take the trash out to the curb.

<u>Wednesday</u>

Yesterday at school, they announced tryouts for the big Winter Talent Show.

As soon as I found out about it, I came up with this AWESOME idea for a comedy skit that me and Rowley could do. But I admit the REAL reason I wrote it was to give myself an excuse to talk to Holly Hills, who is Heather Hills's sister and the most popular girl in my grade.

152

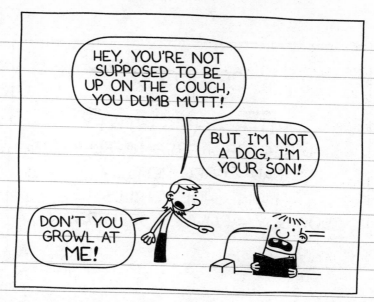

The End.

CREDITS

WRITER - GREG HEFFLEY
DIRECTOR - GREG HEFFLEY
DAD - GREG HEFFLEY
MOM - HOLLY HILLS
DOG-BOY - ROWLEY JEFFERSON

I showed Rowley the script, but he wasn't too enthusiastic about the idea.

You'd think Rowley would be grateful that I was gonna make him a big star. But like Mom always says, there are some people you just can't please.

<u>Thursday</u>
Rowley went and found someone ELSE to partner with for the Talent Show. He's gonna do a magic act with this kid from his karate class named Scotty Douglas.

And if you want to know if I'm jealous, let me put it to you this way: Scotty Douglas is in the FIRST GRADE. So Rowley will be lucky if he doesn't get beat up at school for this.

They're having one big Talent Show for the elementary school, the middle school, and the high school. So that means Rodrick and his band are gonna be in the same competition as Rowley and Scotty Douglas.

Rodrick's ALL fired up about the Talent Show. His band has never played in front of a crowd, so they see this as their big chance to get noticed.

Rodrick is still grounded, but the rule is that he's not allowed to leave the house. So his band just comes over every day and practices down in the basement. I think Dad's starting to wish he had worded Rodrick's punishment a little differently.

BA-DUM BUM
CRASH BAM

But if Rodrick's band really thinks they can win this Talent Show, they better get serious and play some actual music. Because they spent their last two practices fooling around with a new echo pedal they got over the weekend.

SOMEBODY
FARTED FARTED
FARTED FARTED
FARTED

<u>Friday</u>

Dad ended Rodrick's punishment two weeks early, because he was going bonkers listening to Löded Diper practice every day. So tonight, Rodrick went to his friend Ward's for the weekend.

With Rodrick out of the house, that meant the basement was free. So I invited Rowley over to spend the night.

Me and Rowley bought a bunch of candy and soda, and Rowley brought over his portable TV. We even managed to get our hands on a couple of Rodrick's horror movies, so we were all set. But then Mom came downstairs with Manny.

LOOK WHO
CAME TO
JOIN
YOU!

The only reason Mom dumped Manny on us was so he could spy and tell her if we were doing anything wrong.

Every single time I've had a sleepover, Manny has ruined it. The last time Rowley slept over was the WORST.

Manny must've gotten cold in the middle of the night, so he crawled into Rowley's sleeping bag to get warm.

That freaked Rowley out enough to make him go home early. And he hasn't been back to spend the night ever since.

It looked like Manny was gonna ruin ANOTHER
sleepover. Me and Rowley couldn't watch our horror
movies with Manny around, so we decided to just
play board games instead.

But I'm a little sick of board games, and
besides, Rowley was kind of driving me crazy.

He needed to go to the bathroom every five
minutes, and whenever he'd come back downstairs,
he'd kick a pillow across the room.

BOOH-YAH!

KICK

It might have been funny the first couple of times,
but then it really started getting on my nerves. So
the next time Rowley went upstairs to use the
bathroom, I played a prank on him.

159

I put one of Dad's dumbbells underneath a pillow. And sure enough, the next time Rowley came downstairs, he gave it a big kick.

Well, that did it. Rowley started blubbering like a baby, and I couldn't quiet him down.

And with all the racket Rowley was making, Mom came downstairs.

Mom took a look at Rowley's big toe, and she seemed pretty concerned. I think Mom's sensitive about Rowley getting injured in our house after the tinfoil ball incident, so she drove him right home.

I was just glad she didn't ask us how it happened.

As soon as Mom and Rowley walked out the door, I knew I'd better start working on Manny.

Manny saw me put that dumbbell under the pillow, and I knew he would tell Mom what I did. So I came up with an idea to keep him from snitching.

I packed some bags and told Manny I was gonna run away from home so I didn't have to face Mom for what I did.

Then I walked out the door and acted like I was leaving for good.

I got that idea from Rodrick. He used to pull the same kind of thing on me when HE did something bad and he knew I was gonna tell on HIM. He would act like he was running away, and then five minutes later, he would just walk back inside.

And by that time, I was ready to forgive him for whatever he did.

So after I told Manny I was leaving home, I shut the door and waited outside for a few minutes. And when I opened the door, I expected to find him crying in the foyer. But Manny wasn't where I left him. I started walking around the house looking for him, and guess where he was?

Down in the basement, eating my candy.

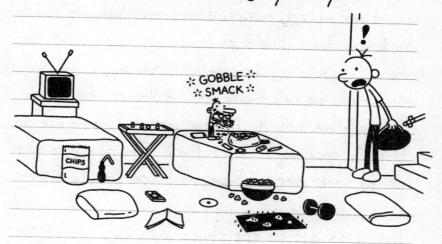

Anyway, if letting Manny eat my candy is the price I have to pay to keep him quiet, I can live with it.

Saturday
After I woke up this morning, I went down to the kitchen. But one look at Mom's face told me that Manny sold me out.

Manny told Mom everything. He even told her about our horror movies. Don't even ask me how he knew about THAT.

Mom made me call Rowley to apologize, but then she made me talk to his parents and apologize to THEM, too. So I don't think I'm going to get invited back over to Rowley's house any time soon.

Then Mom got on the phone with Mrs. Jefferson. Mrs. Jefferson said Rowley's big toe was broken, and that he had to stay off it for a week.

Then Mrs. Jefferson said Rowley is "heartbroken", because this means he'll have to miss the Talent Show tryouts. And he's been practicing his magic act with Scotty Douglas all week.

So Mom told Mrs. Jefferson that I would be HAPPY to fill in for Rowley at the tryouts. I started tugging at Mom's sleeve to let her know this was a TERRIBLE idea, but of course she just ignored me.

After Mom got off the phone, I told her the last thing I needed at school is to be onstage doing magic tricks with a kid who was in pull-ups a year ago.

But Mom made me go through with it anyway. She took me down to Scotty's house and explained the situation to his mother. So now there was no getting out of it.

Mrs. Douglas invited me inside, and me and Scotty went up to his room to start practicing. Well, the first thing I found out was that Rowley and Scotty were not equal partners in this act. Rowley was actually Scotty's ASSISTANT.

I told Scotty there was no WAY I was gonna be a magician's assistant to a first-grader. But Scotty said it was HIS magic set, and he started throwing a big tantrum.

So I just went along with the idea to keep Scotty quiet, because believe me, I did not need any more trouble.

Then Scotty handed me this shirt that was covered with all these sparkly sequins, and he told me that it was my costume.

It looked like something Gramma would wear to Bingo. I told Scotty maybe I could wear something cooler, like a leather jacket, but he said that wouldn't be "magic" enough.

Anyway, it turns out all I have to do for the act is hand Scotty a prop every once in a while, so maybe it really isn't going to be all that bad.

But ask me how I feel again if we get in and have to perform onstage in front of five hundred people instead of Scotty's baby sister.

Sunday
I'll tell you ONE good thing that's come out of practicing this magic act with Scotty Douglas: It's given me a bunch of good ideas for more Creighton the Cretin comics.

Rowley quit doing his comic strip "Zoo-Wee Mama!" for the school paper a few months ago, because he said he wanted to have more time to play with his Dinoblazer action figures. That means the cartoonist job is open again, and maybe I have a shot.

I'M GONNA MAKE THIS APPLE DISAPPEAR.

OH, BOY!

TA DA!

YOU DIDN'T MAKE IT DISAPPEAR, YOU JUST ATE IT!

UH OH, YOU FIGURED OUT MY TRICK.

YOU DIDN'T EVEN EAT THE WHOLE THING!

OK, WATCH THIS. NOW AIN'T **THAT** MAGIC?

THAT'S NOT MAGIC, IT'S JUST A LIGHTER!

FLICK

OOPS. I THOUGHT IT WAS MAGIC.

BOO! YOU'RE NOT A MAGICIAN, YOU'RE AN IDIOT!

PLUS, THAT'S NOT EVEN A MAGICIAN'S HAT. IT'S AN ABRAHAM LINCOLN HAT!

OOPS.

THE END.

Monday
Well, good news on the Talent Show. The tryouts
were today, and me and Scotty didn't make it in.

OK, so maybe I could have done a better job as
Scotty's assistant. But I didn't blow it on
PURPOSE. I just forgot to hand him his
props once or twice.

We were the ONLY ones who didn't make the
cut, and that actually is kind of embarrassing.

I know we weren't exactly the best act trying
out today, but we weren't the WORST, either.
Some of the acts that got in were a lot lamer
than our magic act.

This kindergartner named Harry Gilbertson made the cut, and all he did was roller-skate figure eights around a boom box that was playing "Yankee Doodle Dandy".

Rodrick's band made it in, too, and he's acting like that's some huge accomplishment.

Like I said before, Rodrick is really excited about the Winter Talent Show. In fact, he actually got his Science Fair project done a day EARLY so he could squeeze in some extra band practices before the big night.

But when Rodrick turned in his project, his Science teacher told him he was gonna have to start over and come up with a whole new idea. He said that Rodrick didn't use the "scientific method" with a hypothesis and a conclusion and all that.

Rodrick told the teacher he actually grew a sixteenth of an inch during his "zero gravity" experiment, so that proved he was on to something.

But his teacher said that's a normal amount for a boy Rodrick's age to grow in a month.

Well, this really stinks for me, because I had decided to do my Science Fair project on "zero gravity," too.

And now it looks like all the research I did was just a big waste of time.

Dad told Rodrick he's going to have to just skip the Talent Show so he can do a new experiment, but Rodrick says he's not going to do it.

Rodrick told Dad he doesn't CARE about school anymore. He said his plan is to win the talent show and use the tape of the performance to get signed to a record label. Then he'll quit school and just do the band full-time.

It sounds like a terrible plan to me, but I think Dad is pretty open to the idea.

<u>Wednesday</u>

Tonight was the big Winter Talent Show. I didn't want to go, and neither did Dad. But Mom made us both go to show our support for Rodrick.

Rodrick and Mom went to the school early to bring some stuff that Rodrick's band needed, so Dad had to ride in the band's van with Bill. And Dad wasn't too thrilled when he ran into his boss in the school parking lot.

The show kicked off at 7:00, and let me just say, I think it was a really bad idea to combine the three schools for this thing.

They ended up having kindergartners singing songs to their teddy bears followed by eighteen-year-olds doing speed metal guitar solos.

I don't think Dad approved of Larry Larkin and all his piercings. Halfway through Larry's guitar solo, Dad leaned over and whispered to the man sitting next to him.

I wish I had time to warn Dad that the guy he was talking to was Larry's father.

Another problem with combining the schools was that there were too many acts, and the show went on FOREVER.

At 9:30 they decided to start running two acts at the same time to keep the show moving along. Sometimes it worked out all right, like when they had Patty Farrell tap-dancing while Spencer Kitt was juggling. But other times it didn't work out too good, like when Terrence James played a harmonica on a unicycle while Charise Kline read her poem about global warming.

Rodrick's band was the last act to take the stage.

Before the show, Rodrick asked me to videotape his band during their act, but I told him no WAY.

He's been such a jerk to me lately that I can't believe he was trying to hit me up for a favor. So Mom volunteered for camera duty.

Rodrick's band got paired up with Harry Gilbertson, the roller-skating kid. And I'm sure Rodrick wasn't too happy about THAT.

I noticed Dad wasn't sitting next to me while Rodrick's band played, so I looked around for him.

Dad was standing in the back of the gym with cotton balls sticking out of his ears, and he stayed there until the song was over.

After Rodrick's band performed, they handed out the awards. Rodrick's band didn't win anything, but Harry Gilbertson walked away with the prize for "Best Musical Act".

But you'll never guess who the Grand Prize Winner was: Rowley's babysitter, Leland.

He won for his ventriloquist act, because the judges said it was "wholesome".

I never thought I'd agree with Rodrick on anything, but I'm starting to wonder if maybe he was right about Leland being a nerd after all.

HEY, WHO'S THE DUMMY HERE?

After the show, Rodrick's band came back to our house to watch the videotape of their performance.

They were all grumbling about how they got "robbed", and how the judges don't know the first thing about rock and roll.

178

So their plan was to just mail the videotape off
to some record labels and let their performance
speak for itself.

They all sat down in front of the TV and
Rodrick put the tape in the machine. But it took
about thirty seconds for everyone to realize the
tape was worthless.

You know how Rodrick asked Mom to videotape the
show? Well, she did a pretty good job of filming, but
she talked nonstop during the first two minutes. And
the camera picked up every little comment she made.

THAT SHIRT MAKES
RODRICK'S ARMS LOOK
SO SKINNY!

Every time Bill stuck out his tongue and flicked it up and down like a rock star, you could hear Mom ring in with her opinion.

I DON'T LIKE THAT!

In fact, the only time Mom stopped talking was when Rodrick did his drum solo. But during that part, the camera was shaking around so much that you couldn't even see anything.

At first, Rodrick and his bandmates were really mad. But then one of them remembered that the school taped the Talent Show, and it's supposed to be on the local cable channel tomorrow night.

I guess that means they'll all be coming back over to watch THAT.

Thursday

Well, things have gotten REALLY bad for me in the last few hours.

Rodrick and his bandmates came over around 7:00 tonight to watch the Talent Show on TV. They sat through the whole three-hour show until their band came on.

The school actually did a decent job of taping the performance, and things were looking pretty good up until Rodrick's drum solo.

That's when Mom started dancing. And whoever was doing the filming zoomed right in on Mom, and kept the camera pointed at her for the rest of the song.

That meant Rodrick didn't have ANYTHING he could send to record companies. And he was really mad about it, too.

At first he was mad at Mom for messing things up. But Mom said that if Rodrick didn't want people to dance, he shouldn't play music.

Then Rodrick turned on ME. He said this was all MY fault, because if I just taped the show like he asked me to, none of this would've happened.

But I told him that maybe if he wasn't such a jerk, I would have done it for him.

We started to yell at each other. Mom and Dad broke us up, and then they sent Rodrick down to his room and me up to mine.

But a couple of hours later I went downstairs, and I ran into Rodrick in the kitchen. He was smiling, so I knew something was up.

Rodrick told me my "secret was out".

At first, I didn't know what he was talking about. But then I got it: He was talking about the thing that happened to me this summer.

I ran down to the basement, and I picked up Rodrick's phone to see if he had made any calls. And sure enough, it looked like he had called EVERY friend of his who had a brother or sister my age.

By tomorrow morning, EVERYONE at my school will know the story. And I'm sure Rodrick exaggerated the facts to make the story sound even WORSE.

Now that my secret's out there, I want to put on record what REALLY happened, and not Rodrick's twisted version.

So here it goes.

Over the summer, me and Rodrick had to stay with Grandpa at his condo in Leisure Towers for a few days. But there was NOTHING to do, and I was going bonkers.

I was so bored, I broke out my old journal and started to write in it. But taking out a book that said "diary" on the cover in front of Rodrick was a HUGE mistake.

Rodrick stole my journal and made a run for it.
He probably would have made it into the bathroom
and locked the door if someone hadn't left
Gutbusters sitting out.

I scooped the book off the floor and ran out
into the hallway and down the stairwell. Then,
I ducked into the bathroom in the main lobby
and locked myself in a stall.

I kept my feet off the floor so that if Rodrick
came in, he wouldn't know I was in there.

I knew that if Rodrick got ahold of my journal, it
would be a nightmare. So I decided to just rip the
whole thing into tiny little pieces and flush them
down the toilet. It was better to just destroy the
thing than risk Rodrick getting his hands on it.

But as soon as I started ripping pages out of the book, I heard the bathroom door open. I thought it was Rodrick, so I just stayed completely still.

I didn't hear anything, so I peeked over the top of the stall to see what was going on. That's when I saw a woman standing in front of the mirror, putting on makeup.

I figured the lady just accidentally wandered into the men's room, because people at Leisure Towers are always doing stuff like that.

I was about to speak up and tell this lady she was in the wrong bathroom, but right then someone else walked in. And guess what? It was ANOTHER woman.

That's when I realized that I was the one who messed up, and I was in the WOMEN's bathroom.

I prayed that those ladies would just wash their hands and leave so I could make a run for it. But they sat down in the stalls on either side of me. And every time one woman would leave the bathroom, someone else would come in and take their place. So I couldn't leave.

If Rowley thinks he had it bad when those kids made him eat the Cheese, he should try being stuck in the Leisure Towers ladies' room for an hour and a half.

I guess someone eventually heard me in there, and they reported me to the front desk. Within a few minutes, word got around the building that there was a "Peeping Tom" in the women's room.

By the time security came in and got me out of there, everyone who lived in Leisure Towers was down in the lobby. And Rodrick saw the whole thing unfold upstairs on Grandpa's TV.

Now that the story was out, I knew I couldn't show my face at school. So I told Mom she was gonna have to transfer me somewhere else, and I told her why.

Mom said I shouldn't worry about what other people think. She told me that my classmates would understand that I had just made an "honest mistake".

So that just proves once and for all that Mom doesn't understand a THING about kids my age.

Now I'm kicking myself for not keeping up my pen-pal relationship with Mamadou. Because if me and him had stayed in touch, maybe I could have gone to France as an exchange student and hid out THERE for a few years.

All I know is, the one place I don't want to go tomorrow is school. And it looks like that's exactly where I'm headed.

Friday

The CRAZIEST thing happened today. When I walked in the door at school, a bunch of guys cornered me, and I braced myself for the teasing to start. But instead of harassing me, they started CONGRATULATING me.

Everyone was shaking my hand and patting me on the back, and I didn't know WHAT was going on.

With all those guys talking to me at the same time, it took me a while to make sense of anything. But here's what must have happened.

The story Rodrick told his friends got passed on to their brothers and sisters, and then they told THEIR friends.

But by the time word spread around, all the details got totally messed up.

So the story went from me accidentally walking into the women's bathroom at Leisure Towers to me infiltrating the girls' locker room at Crossland HIGH SCHOOL.

I couldn't believe everything got twisted like that, but I wasn't about to set the record straight, either.

All of the sudden, I was the hero at school. I even got a nickname. People were calling me the "Stealthinator".

Someone even made me a Stealthinator headband, and you better believe I wore it. Things like this NEVER happen to me, so I wasn't gonna pass up my moment of glory.

And for the first time ever, I knew what it felt like to be the most popular kid at school.

Unfortunately, the girls weren't as impressed with me as the guys were. In fact, I think I might have a little trouble getting someone to go to the Valentine's Dance with me.

<u>Monday</u>
You know how Rodrick wanted his band to get
noticed? Well, he kind of got his wish, because
EVERYBODY knows who Löded Diper is now.

I guess somebody must have thought the tape of
Mom cutting loose at the Talent Show was pretty
funny, because it's all over the Internet. And
now everyone knows Rodrick Heffley as the drummer
from the "Dancing Mom" video.

Ever since, Rodrick's been hiding out in the
basement, waiting for the whole thing to blow
over. And I have to admit, I do feel kind of
sorry for him.

I'm getting teased about the video at school,
too, but at least I'm not IN it.

194

And even though Rodrick can be a huge jerk sometimes, he IS my brother.

Tomorrow is the Science Fair, and if Rodrick doesn't turn in a project, he's gonna flunk out of school.

So that's why I offered to help him out with his project, but just this one last time. We worked together all night, and I don't mean to brag, but we did a really good job.

Anyway, when Rodrick gets First Prize tomorrow and passes Science, I just hope he realizes how lucky he is to have a brother like ME.

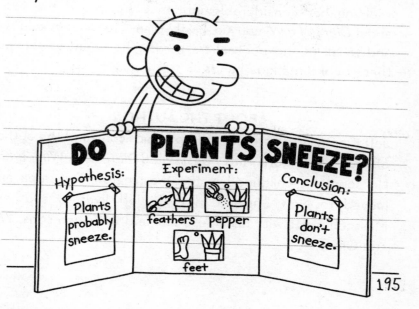

ACKNOWLEDGMENTS

I'll be forever grateful to my family for providing the inspiration, encouragement, and support I need to create these books. A huge thanks goes to my brothers, Scott and Pat; my sister, Re; and to my mom and dad. Without you, there would be no Heffleys. Thanks to my wife, Julie, and my kids, who have made so many sacrifices to make my dream of being a cartoonist come true. Thanks also to my in-laws, Tom and Gail, who have been there with a helping hand during every deadline.

Thanks to the terrific folks at Abrams, especially Charlie Kochman, an incredibly dedicated editor and a remarkable human being, and to those people at Abrams with whom I've had the pleasure of working most closely: Jason Wells, Howard Reeves, Susan Van Metre, Chad Beckerman, Samara Klein, Valerie Ralph, and Scott Auerbach. A special thanks goes to Michael Jacobs.

Thanks to Jess Brallier for bringing Greg Heffley to the world on Funbrain.com. Thanks to Betsy Bird (Fuse #8) for wielding her considerable influence to spread the word about *Diary of a Wimpy Kid*. Lastly, thanks to Dee Sockol-Frye, and to all of the booksellers across the country who put these books into kids' hands.

ABOUT THE AUTHOR

Jeff Kinney is the creator of Poptropica.com, and the author of the #1 *New York Times* bestseller *Diary of a Wimpy Kid*. He spent his childhood in the Washington, D.C. area and moved to New England in 1995. Jeff lives in southern Massachusetts with his wife, Julie, and their two sons, Will and Grant.

杰夫·金尼 中国行

Jeff Kinney's Visit to China

2015年对中国的"哈屁族"来说，是具有划时代意义的一年！因为《小屁孩日记》的作者杰夫·金尼终于掘出了他童年梦想中的那条地道，从美国到地球另一边的中国来啦！

北京是"杰夫·金尼2015全球巡回活动"的第4站。2015年11月4日，以扁平娃斯坦利为首的一众小编终于在北京首都国际机场迎来了"小屁孩之父"杰夫·金尼！

主角登场！

接下来的11月5日，重头戏轮番上演啦！

★ 杰夫叔叔先是参加了《小屁孩日记》中文版发行600万册的庆祝会，并在会上宣布了他的新书出版计划。

大家要关注《小屁孩日记》的新书哟！

中国儿童文学作家颜值都那么高吗？（设计对白）

★ 然后，他跟中国著名儿童文学作家"阳光姐姐"伍美珍就中美少儿课外阅读情况展开了对谈。

杰夫叔叔原来也好亲切呀！（设计对白）

★ 活动现场也来了很多"哈屁族"，自然少不了签书环节，《小屁孩日记》真是大小通吃呢！

★ 不少书迷一拿到书就迫不及待地看了起来，你看，头都要扎到书里去啦！

★ 杰夫叔叔还收获了"哈屁族"送的一大堆礼物。这位小读者好有心思呀，让杰夫叔叔认识了自己的中文名。

★ 11月5日下午，杰夫叔叔还到当当网的总部接受了访谈，回答了很多有趣的问题，例如：

主持人 通过今天上午的接触，您觉得中国的小读者跟您想象的小读者是一样的吗？

我觉得全球的孩子都是一样的，他们都有父母、兄弟姐妹、有宠物和老师，所以这就是我的书为什么能受到这些孩子欢迎的原因，因为世界各地的孩子们的童年是有很多共通之处的。

主持人 因为这本书里面的事情太逼真了，会让人觉得很多事情是不是发生在您自己小时候，或者发生在您孩子的身上？

这些故事大部分其实都是有一些真人真事的依据的，然后根据这些事进行的改编。比如说我刚才随手翻开一页，这一页描述的是，格雷在院子里面找他祖母的戒指。这个故事确有其事……

篇幅有限，未能尽录。

好玩的问题还有很多呢，大家一定还想看看杰夫叔叔的回答吧？不要着急，只要关注"新世纪童书绘"的微信公众号（搜索"xsjpublish"，或扫描右手边的二维码），在对话框输入"小屁孩"并发送，就可以看到这次访谈的全部内容啦！

★ 11月5日晚上，杰夫叔叔来到北京西单图书大厦，跟广大读者见面，还给大家示范了"小屁孩"格雷的画法。

★ 活动结束后，杰夫叔叔还没能休息哦！他被带到一堆"书山"前面，这是要干什么呢？

当然是为广大读者谋福利啦！你们想要的亲笔签名本，就是从这个"深夜流水线"上扒下来的。

立刻关注全国各大书店及各大网络书店的动态，即有机会获得杰夫·金尼亲笔签名的《小屁孩日记》。

★ 11月6日，杰夫叔叔终于如愿来到了神秘又古老的故宫。

好兴奋！可以跟杰夫叔叔同游故宫耶！（设计对白）

好兴奋！终于到故宫啦！（设计对白）

又被读者逮住索要签名了。

跟扁平娃斯坦利来张合照吧！茄子！

杰夫叔叔短短两天的中国之旅就这样愉快地结束啦！你们想再见到他吗？想他到你的城市去吗？赶快关注"新世纪童书绘"的微信公众号（搜索"xsjpublish"，或扫描前页的二维码）和"小屁孩日记官方微博"（http://weibo.com/wimpywimpy），或者打电话到020-83795744，把你们的愿望告诉小编吧！

望子快乐

朱子庆

在一个人的一生中，"与有荣焉"的机会或有，但肯定不多。因为儿子译了一部畅销书，而老爸被邀涂鸦几句，像这样的与荣，我想，即使放眼天下，也没有几人领得吧。

儿子接活儿翻译《小屁孩日记》时，还在读着大三。这是安安他第一次领译书稿，多少有点紧张和兴奋吧，起初他每译几段，便"飞鸽传书"，不一会儿人也跟过来，在我面前"项庄舞剑"地问："有意思么？有意思么？"怎么当时我就没有作乐不可支状呢？于今想来，我竟很有些后悔。对于一个喂饱段子与小品的中国人，若说还有什么洋幽默能令我们"绝倒"，难！不过，安安译成杀青之时，图文并茂，我得以从头到尾再读一遍，我得当说，这部书岂止有意思呢，读了它使我有一种冲动，假如时间可以倒流，我很想尝试重新做一回父亲！我不免窃想，安安在译它的时候，不知会怎样腹诽我这个老爸呢！

我宁愿儿子是书里那个小屁孩！

你可能会说，你别是在做秀吧，小屁孩格雷将来能出息成个什么样子，实在还很难说……这个质疑，典型地出诸一个中国人之口，出之于为父母的中国人之口。望子成龙，一定要孩子出息成个什么样子，虽说初衷也是为了孩子，但最终却是苦了孩子。"生年不满百，常怀千岁忧。"现在，由于这深重的忧患，我们已经把成功学启示的模式都做到胎教了！而望子快乐，有谁想过？从小就快乐，快乐一生？惭愧，我也是看了《小屁孩日记》才想到这点，然而儿子已不再年少！我觉得很有些对不住儿子！

我从来没有对安安的"少年老成"感到过有什么不妥，毕竟少年老成使人放心。而今读其译作而被触动，此心才为之不安起来。我在想，比起美国的小屁孩格雷和他的同学们，我们中国的小屁孩们是不是活得不很小屁孩？是不是普遍地过于负重、乏乐和少年老成？而当他们将来长大，娶妻（嫁夫）生子（女），为人父母，会不会还要循此逻辑再造下一代？想想安安少年时，起早贪黑地读书、写作业，小四眼，十足一个书呆子，类似格雷那样的调皮、贪玩、小有恶搞、缰绳牢笼不住地敢于尝试和行动主义……太缺少了。印象中，安安最突出的一次，也就是读小学三年级时，做了一回带头大哥，拔了校园里所有自行车的气门芯并四处派发，仅此而已吧（此处请在家长指导下阅读）。

说点别的吧。中国作家写的儿童文学作品，很少能引发成年读者的阅读兴趣。安徒生童话之所以风靡天下，在于它征服了成年读者。在我看来，《小屁孩日记》也属于成人少年兼宜的读物，可以父子同修！谁没有年少轻狂？谁没有豆蔻年华？只不过呢，对于为父母者，阅读它，会使你由会心一笑而再笑，继以感慨系之，进而不免有所自省，对照和检讨一下自己和孩子的关系，以及在某些类似事情的处理上，自己是否欠妥？等等。它虽系成人所作，书中对孩子心性的把握，却准确传神；虽非心理学著作，对了解孩子的心理和行为，也不无参悟和启示。品学兼优和顽劣不学的孩子毕竟是少数，小屁孩格雷是"中间人物"的一个玲珑典型，着实招人怜爱——在格雷身上，有着我们彼此都难免有的各样小心思、小算计、小毛病，就好像阿Q，读来透着与我们有那么一种割不断的血缘关系，这，也许就是此书在美国乃至全球都特别畅销的原因吧！

最后我想申明的是，第一读者身份在我是弥足珍惜的，因为，宝贝儿子出生时，第一眼看见他的是医生，老爸都摊不上第一读者呢！

我眼中的 ......

好书，爱不释手！

★ 读者 王汐子（女，2009年留学美国，攻读大学传媒专业）《小屁孩日记》在美国掀起的阅读风潮可不是盖的，在我留学美国的这一年中，不止一次目睹这套书对太平洋彼岸人民的巨大影响。高速公路上巨大的广告宣传牌就不用说了，我甚至在学校书店买课本时看到了这套书被大大咧咧地摆上书架，"小屁孩"的搞笑日记就这样理直气壮地充当起了美国大学生的课本教材！为什么这套书如此受欢迎？为什么一个普普通通的小男孩能让这么多成年人捧腹大笑？也许可以套用一个万能句式"每个人心中都有一个XXX"。每个人心中都有一个小屁孩，每个人小时候也有过这样的时光，每天都有点鸡毛蒜皮的小烦恼，像作业这么多怎么办啦，要考试了书都没有看怎么办啦……但是大部分时候还是因为调皮捣蛋被妈妈教训……就这样迷迷糊糊地走过了"小屁孩"时光，等长大后和朋友们讨论后才恍然大悟，随即不禁感慨，原来那时候我们都一样呀……是呀，全世界的小屁孩都一样！

★ 读者 zhizhimother（发表于2009-06-12）在杂志上看到这书的介绍，一时冲动在当当上下了单，没想到，一买回来一家人抢着看，笑得前仰后合。我跟女儿一人抢到一本，老公很不满意，他嘟囔着下一本出的时候他要第一个看。看多了面孔雷同的好孩子的书，看到这本，真是深有感触，我们的孩子其实都是这样长大的！

轻松阅读　捧腹大笑

★　这是著名的畅销书作家小巫的儿子Sam口述的英语和中文读后感：我喜欢《小屁孩日记》，因为Greg是跟我们一样的普通孩子。他的故事很好玩儿，令我捧腹大笑，他做的事情很搞笑，有点儿傻乎乎的。书里的插图也很幽默。

★　读者　dearm暖baby（发表于2009-07-29）我12岁了，过生日时妈妈给我买了这样两本书，真的很有趣！一半是中文，一半是英文，彻底打破了"英文看不懂看下面中文"的局限！而且这本书彻底地给我来了次大放松，"重点中学"的压力也一扫而光！总之，两个字：超赞！

孩子爱上写日记了！

★　读者　ddian2003（发表于2009-12-22）正是于丹的那几句话吸引我买下了这套书。自己倒没看，但女儿却用了三天学校的课余时间就看完了，随后她大受启发，连着几天都写了日记。现在这书暂时搁在书柜里，已和女儿约定，等她学了英文后再来看一遍，当然要看书里的英文了。所以这书还是买得物有所值的。毕竟女儿喜欢！！

做个"不听话的好孩子"

★　读者　水真爽（发表于2010-03-27）这套书是买给我上小学二年级的儿子的。有时候他因为到该读书的时间而被要求从网游下来很恼火。尽管带着气，甚至眼泪，可是读起这本书来，总是能被书中小屁孩的种种淘气出格行为和想法弄得哈哈大笑。书中的卡通漫画也非常不错。这种文字漫画形式的日记非常具有趣味性，老少咸宜。对低年级孩子或爱画漫画的孩子尤其有启发作用。更重要的是提醒家长们要好好留意观察这些"不怎么听话"的小屁孩们的内心世界，他们的健康成长需要成人的呵护引导，但千万不要把他们都变成只会"听大人话"的好孩子。

对照《小屁孩日记》分享育儿体验

★ 读者 gjrzj2002@＊＊＊.＊＊＊（发表于2010-05-21）看完四册书，我想着自己虽然不可能有三个孩子，但一个孩子的成长经历至今仍记忆犹新。儿子还是幼儿的时候，比较像曼尼，在爸妈眼中少有缺点，真是让人越看越爱，想要什么就基本上能得到什么。整个幼儿期父母对孩子肯定大过否定。上了小学，儿子的境地就不怎么从容了，上学的压力时时处处在影响着他，小家伙要承受各方面的压力，父母、老师、同学，太过我行我素、大而化之都是行不通的，比如没写作业的话，老师、家长的批评和提醒是少不了的，孩子在慢慢学着适应这种生活，烦恼也随之而来，这一阶段比较像格雷，虽然儿子的思维还没那么丰富，快乐和烦恼的花样都没那么多，但处境差不多，表扬和赞美不像以前那样轻易就能得到了。儿子青年时代会是什么样子我还不得而知，也不可想象，那种水到渠成的阶段要靠前面的积累，我希望自己到时候能平心静气，坦然接受，无论儿子成长成什么样子。

气味相投的好伙伴

★ 上海市外国语大学附属第一实验中学，中预10班，沈昕仪Elaine：《小屁孩日记》读来十分轻松。虽然没有用十分华丽的语言，却使我感受到了小屁孩那缤纷多彩的生活，给我带来无限的欢乐。那精彩的插图、幽默的文字实在是太有趣了，当中的故事在我们身边都有可能发生，让人身临其境。格雷总能说出我的心里话，他是和我有着共同语言的朋友。所以他们搞的恶作剧一直让我跃跃欲试，也想找一次机会尝试一下。不知道别的读者怎么想，我觉得格雷挺喜欢出风头的。我也是这样的人，总怕别人无视自己。当看到格雷蹦出那些稀奇古怪的点子的时候，我多想帮他一把啊——毕竟我们是"气味相投"的同类人嘛。另一方面，我身处在外语学校，时刻都需要积累英语单词，但这件事总是让我觉得枯燥乏味。而《小屁孩日记》帮了我的大忙：我在享受快乐阅读的同时，还可以对照中英文学到很多常用英语单词。我发现其实生活中还有很多事情值得我们去用笔写下来。即使是小事，这些童年的故事也是很值得我们回忆的。既然还生活在童年，还能够写下那些故事，又何乐而不为呢？

画出我心中的"小屁孩"

邓博笔下的赫夫利一家

读者@童_Cc.与@曲奇做的"小屁孩"手抄报

　　亲爱的读者，你看完这本书后，有什么感想吗？请来电或是登录本书的博客与我们分享吧！等本书再版时，这里也许换上了你的读后感呢！

　　我们的电话号码是：020-83795744；博客地址是：blog.sina.com.cn/wimpykid；微博地址是：weibo.com/wimpywimpy。